Merry Merry Merry Murder

Cuddle Farm Mystery
Book 1

Paty Jager
Windtree Press

MERRY MERRY MERRY MURDER

Contact Information: info@windtreepress.com

Windtree Press
Hillsboro, Oregon
http://windtreepress.com

Cover Art by Covers by Karen

PUBLISHING HISTORY
Published in the United States of America
ISBN 978-1940064-10-9

The idea for this book came to me when someone suggested that my little dog, Nia, a Chihuahua/Dachshund cross, would be a good therapy dog.

I didn't have time to take her around to help others but I did have the imagination and time to write a book about a group of therapy animals and their owner who help others not only with mental health but by solving murders.

I hope you enjoy the Cuddle Farm Mysteries.

Chapter One

Driving up to Auburn City Park, I felt the same bubbles of excitement I had as a child. The Christmas Festival, held on the Saturday after Thanksgiving, marks the beginning of the holiday season in our small town of Auburn. Everyone from our community and nearby small towns came to shop at the craft and homemade food booths, and let the kids tell Santa what they want for Christmas.

This all happens in the City Park. The center of town, where every outdoor event is held, other than the rodeo. After a full day of activities in the park, everyone will gather around the largest tree and watch as the Christmas lights are lit.

I smiled, parking the van in front of the sandwich board that announced the time Santa would be available for photos, to sit on his lap, and tell him your Christmas wishes. My fourth Christmas rushed back to me as if I were the small child jogging up and down in place, fearing I wouldn't get my chance to see Santa.

My pregnant mom, Nina, my older sister by five years, and I were setting up the booth where our family sold wool, yarn, and garments from the sheep we raised. Daddy couldn't help set up because there had been coyotes in the sheep herd the night before. Nina and Mom were both impatient with my whining about visiting Santa and not bringing them the items they asked for.

That's when Blind Betty, an adopted Ethiopian girl two years older than me, came by the booth and asked if one of us could take her to see Santa. I thought it was funny because she couldn't really see him and laughed.

Mom said, "Andrea Hazel Weber, you apologize to Betty and take her along to the Santa booth."

I couldn't get moving fast enough. I grabbed Betty's hand and dragged her across the park to the pavilion, where Santa's sleigh sat in the center, being used as the backdrop for the photos. From that day forward, Betty and I became friends. She nicknamed me Andi, and I've gone by that ever since.

"That was one of the best days of my life," I say, shifting in my seat and smiling at the three dogs in the middle seat. They all smile back at me. Or I like to think they were smiling. I know their eyes were bright with anticipation of the people they'd meet today.

Peering forward, I watched people bustling around getting food and craft booths ready for the event to kick off in an hour. There were faces I remembered from all those years ago. Or maybe it wasn't the faces so much as the booths, and then recognizing the aged faces.

My stomach did a little wobble. This was my first time back in twenty years. After graduating high school, I went to college, fell in love, and married Mick, who took me all over the world. We only came back to Auburn for one-week stays in between his jobs, which was never during the winter.

Coming back to Auburn had been my first thought when I got over the shock of my husband dying in a freak accident. And this. The people, the community involvement, and feeling as if I belonged were why I didn't think twice about going anywhere else.

People called out to one another, slapped acquaintances on the back, and all seemed as excited as I'd felt as a four-year-old. The whole county was eager to move from the doldrums of a rainy fall into preparations for Christmas. It helped that it was the Saturday after Thanksgiving, and many needed the exercise to work off all they had eaten on Thursday.

With only an hour before the event started, I needed to stop reminiscing and get busy. I never arrive more than an hour before an event. Any earlier, my crew of cuddles would become bored and get into trouble. The committee asked me to set up a small petting zoo at the entrance to the holiday event. I scanned the inflatable decorations and roped-off areas that would funnel attendees down a specific path through all the booths and over to where Santa would listen to children's Christmas wishes and spotted our sign.

"Come on, Cocoa, I can use your help carrying things." I unsnapped my brown and white border collie from the seatbelt harness and listened to Lulu whine. Scratching the dapple head and soft, long, black furry ears of my Chiweenie, I said, "You're too small to help me right now. You keep Athena company." I patted the blonde head of Athena, my Golden Retriever/Pyrenees, and followed Cocoa to the trailer behind the van.

Luckily, all my animals are small, except for Athena, and fairly easy to handle. Athena is larger than both my mini donkey and pygmy goat. At the trailer loaded with panels to set up a small pen, I pointed to the bucket full of pins that hold the panels together. Cocoa grabbed the handle in her mouth. I gathered the top two panels and carried them to the area with a sign, *Cuddle Farm Animals*.

Cocoa followed with the bucket.

"Good girl." I patted Cocoa's head and told her to stay while I went back to make four more trips. Once all ten panels were in the area, I assembled them with the pins Cocoa brought to me.

"That's a handy dog," a voice behind me said.

Twisting my neck, I caught sight of a man carrying a red Santa suit. "She's my best helper. But she wouldn't make a good elf. She doesn't like to wear pointy shoes and hats."

The man laughed and hurried along the path to the covered pavilion where Santa would greet his fans.

Sliding the last pin in place, I straightened and walked to the van to retrieve Lulu and Athena. Lulu put her nose to the ground, making circles as she followed the different scents. Athena lumbered over to where the pen was set up and lay down, crossing her front legs and scanning the activity around her.

I returned to the back of the van, opened the doors, and pulled out Flopsie, the brown and white Holland lop bunny's cage, and then Chicklet's cage. A brown and tan checkerboard silky hen.

Carrying the two small cages over to the large enclosure, I wished I'd brought my garden wagon. It would have saved half the trips. After depositing the two small cages next to Athena, I returned to the van. Opening the divider between the back where the bunny and hen had been, I snapped lead ropes onto the halters of Sparky, a tan paint mini donkey, and Cupcake, a black and white pygmy goat.

Cupcake jumped out of the back of the van and kicked up her heels, dancing around. Her usual antics when she was released from an enclosed area. Sparky let out a staccato squeaky heee-hee-haw in opposition to jumping out of the van. I handed Cupcake's lead rope to Cocoa and lowered the ramp. Sparky walked down and stood showing off his yellow teeth as I put the ramp up and closed the doors.

After settling the donkey, goat, and Athena in the pen Cocoa and I built, I placed Flopsie and Chicklet's locked cages in the middle so no one walking by could pick them up and walk off. Athena would keep people from trying to get inside the large pen.

"Come on, Cocoa and Lulu. Let's go get some hot chocolate and donuts." I snapped the leashes on the two dogs and we walked down the path to the food booths.

"Andi! Andi!" called a voice I knew well. Following the sound, I found Mom standing in the Weber Wool booth. Colorful knitted scarves, hats, and mittens, as well as woven blankets, covered the shelves and walls.

"Hi, Mom. I thought Nina was going to help you set up?" Since moving back to Auburn, I'd become the business's bookkeeper to help the family business when I'm not running my therapy animals to schools, hospitals, and nursing homes. Nina was in partnership with Mom and my younger brother, Rudy.

"She's getting me a cup of coffee and one of Jeanne's pastries. Are you and your crew all set?" Mom reached down, patting both Cocoa and Lulu on their heads.

"Yes. Athena is watching over the others while I get hot chocolate and donuts." A pretty teal and lavender hat caught my eye. They were my favorite colors. "Any chance you could keep this back for me?" I said, running my hand over the soft hat.

Mom smiled. "I told your sister you'd want that hat when it was finished. But she insisted we had to sell it. Christmas was far enough away that I could make another one." She grabbed the hat off the pile and handed it to me. "Don't wear it around your sister until after Christmas."

I hugged Mom. "I'll try to remember. But it is my two favorite colors." I tucked the hat in my coat pocket and hurried to Jeanne's booth. Jeanne Léon owned the bakery in town. Even if there had been more than her bakery in Auburn, everyone would go to hers. She made the lightest eclairs and puff pastry. Her husband, Peter, made the fluffiest donuts I've ever eaten. They could have made a fortune in a large city with their bakery, but they preferred the slow, laid-back life of Auburn in Eastern Oregon.

Nina walked toward me. "Is your herd ready to wow the kids?"

I hated how Nina made fun of my animals and how they helped people, but then I didn't understand how anyone could be so obsessed with getting a color just right on a skein of yarn or fussing over a pattern that didn't come out right. I didn't get the creative genes from Mom. I received my father's genes. He was, and I still am, interested in animal husbandry and have a knack for numbers.

"The animals are ready. I'm after hot chocolate and donuts to fortify us." I led Cocoa and Lulu by my sister.

"Are you feeding donuts to those poor animals?" Nina asked, her tone filled with disapproval.

I stopped, pivoted toward her, and smiled before saying, "No. The donuts are for the 4-H club that's coming to help me."

"Oh, good. I'd hate to think you feed your animals stuff they shouldn't have." Nina spun on her heel, juggling two cups of coffee and a small white bag with the J & P Bakery logo.

I waited for her to get far enough away and said to Cocoa and Lulu, "You two better not tell her that I give you dessert every night." Both animals looked up with complete innocence in their big brown eyes.

"Good. Let's buy those donuts and get back."

❄ ❄ ❄

Six hours later, I finished thanking the 4-H club for helping out and walked back to the entry of the petting zoo pen. A soft voice came from over where Athena was lying. Dark curly hair flowed over Athena's shoulder. A child in a green coat and black pants lay alongside the dog. The child's pink boots were toes up.

"Athena, I know you won't say anything to anyone. But I'm so confused. I saw Mommy behind Santa's sleigh kissing Santa. Not like she kisses Grandpa on the cheek. She was kissing him like she used to kiss Daddy. Santa might be a good person cuz he gives out presents, but Mommy shouldn't be kissing him. She should be kissing Daddy. I don't know what to do or who to tell. I do know I'm writing Santa a letter and telling him to leave my mommy alone."

My heart went out to the child. Her mother obviously thought she was hidden, but the child had seen something she shouldn't have. I didn't want the child to know I'd heard what she said. I called out, "Are you Cuddle Farm animals ready to go home?"

The child sat up beside Athena. That's when I recognized her. She and her father had visited the wool shop a couple of weeks before. He had black sheep and wanted to know if we would purchase the wool from the sheep. Chef, no, Sheffield had been the last name.

"Hi! Didn't you and your dad come into the Weber Wool shop a while back?" I asked.

The child smiled. "Yes, Daddy said the black sheep should be worth something to someone."

"Hi, I'm Andi." I held out my hand and shook hands with the child.

"I'm Ava. I met Athena at the school last spring." The child patted Athena's wide, flat head.

"She is big and lovable," I agreed. "You want to help me put them in my van?"

The child's eyes widened and a smile spread across her face. "Can I?"

"Sure." I walked over to the tote that held the feed, water, lead ropes, and leashes. "Do you want to lead Sparky or Cupcake?"

"Cupcake, please." Ava held out her hand for the lead rope.

I placed it in her hand, and we walked into the pen. The animals knew the routine. They walked up and allowed the lead ropes to be snapped on. "When we get out of the pen, Cupcake may dance around. It's just her happy dance to be going home. Keep a good grip on the rope so she doesn't get away and follow her as she dances."

Cupcake didn't disappoint. Two families leaving the event stopped to watch and laugh at the tiny goat as she danced over to the van with Ava skipping behind her.

"Hold Sparky while I lower the ramp," I said, handing the lead rope to the child. It was rare that the goat or the donkey ever took off. I was comfortable having Ava hold the two. They'd had a long day and were ready to go home, eat hay, and rest.

We loaded the two and went back for the bunny and chicken cages. "You carry Chicklet, she's lighter than Flopsie."

"Why does she have funny feathers?" Ava asked, picking up the cage and staring at the chicken who bobbed her head, making the tan feathers sticking out all over her head shake. "How does she see? I can't find her eyes."

"She sees better than you'd think," I said, shoving the cages into the back of the van. Once the cages were arranged, I pushed the ramp in and closed the door. "I'll take the panels down, and you can put Lulu and Athena in the middle seat. Make sure you use the leash on the seat belt to hold them in the seats." I wasn't worried about Athena jumping back out, but Lulu was curious and liked to explore.

"What about Cocoa?" Ava asked, patting the border collie's head.

"She'll help me." I handed the pin bucket to Cocoa. She grasped the handle in her mouth and followed along as I pulled the pins out of the panels and dropped them in the bucket. When the pen was dismantled, Rudy walked up.

"Need help?" He picked up two of the panels under one arm and two more under the other.

"I can always use help at the end of the day." I grabbed two panels, one under each arm. We carried them back to the van, where Ava stood petting Athena and Lulu.

"Looks like you have a groupie," Rudy said.

"What's a groupie?" Ava asked.

"It's someone who follows singers or actors around everywhere they go," I said, giving Rudy a stern look.

"I don't follow you around." Ava stood with her hands on her hips. "That's rude to do. Mommy said so."

"My brother didn't mean what he said. He didn't know you were helping me." I wondered why Mrs. Sheffield would need to tell someone they were rude for following her or someone else around.

"You can go now, Ava." I pulled a five-dollar bill out of my pocket and handed it to the child. "Thank you for helping me put the animals in the van."

"Wow! This is for me?" The child's face beamed.

"Yes. You were a big help. Now my brother is here to help me finish loading the panels." At that moment, he arrived with the last four panels under his arms.

"Thanks!" Ava took off running down the sidewalk.

"Where do you think she's going to spend that?" Rudy asked.

"I don't know, but I turned her day around. That's what matters." I straightened the panels on the trailer. "If you go grab the totes, I'll buy you pizza for dinner."

"A large Everything But The Kitchen Sink?" he asked.

"If that's what you want."

"Deal!" Rudy jogged back to where the pen had been set up and returned with the two totes. Once it was all tied down, I told him. "Come to my house in thirty minutes."

"See you there."

I climbed into the van. As I pulled away from the curb, the man from the morning, who had rushed by with a Santa suit over his arm, strode out onto the sidewalk without a Santa suit and an angry face that made me wonder how he could have been picked as Santa.

Chapter Two

"Want to go to the tree lighting tonight?" Rudy asked as he leaned back in his chair after eating all but two pieces of a large Everything But The Kitchen Sink pizza.

I'd eaten the two pieces before Rudy devoured the rest. I sipped my white wine and debated about going back out. The day had been chilly but tolerable. Tonight would be colder, but I'd only be standing in the cold for about an hour, not seven hours. This would be my first tree lighting since I moved back. I remembered the awe and thrill as a child watching the town Christmas tree light up. The festival and lights always put me in the holiday spirit. Something that had been hard for me since losing Mick.

"Why not? It won't feel like Christmas is coming without witnessing the tree lighting." I picked up the empty pizza box and shoved it in the recycle bin. Cocoa nudged my thigh with her nose.

"You want to go?" I scratched her head.

Cocoa danced on her two front paws.

I glanced over at Athena and Lulu curled up together on a large dog bed. It appeared they were through for the day.

"Okay, you can go." As Cocoa went to the hall tree and grabbed her leash, I asked Rudy, "Will you drive? I don't want to try to find a parking spot for the van."

"Sure. We'll both be coming back to the farm anyway. But if I run into Monica, you're driving yourself home or catching a ride with someone." Rudy had been in love with Monica in high school, but she'd married someone from college. After her divorce, she moved back to Auburn, and Rudy was determined to make a family with her and her two teenage children.

"I'm sure Mom or Nina and David will be at the tree lighting. I can catch a ride back here with them." That was the good thing about being involved in the family business. We all lived on the sheep farm. Nina and her husband, David, and their son, Todd, lived in the main farmhouse. Mom and Rudy lived in what had been the shepherd's house. It was the perfect size for them.

When Mick died, I moved back to the ranch, building a small two-bedroom bungalow in a meadow halfway between the county road and the ranch house. I have my privacy, but I'm close by to help when needed. And the farm has room for my therapy animals. A large, carved, wooden sign with the words CUDDLE FARM and images of my animals stands at the entrance to my property.

I pulled on a warmer coat than I'd worn during the day and started to put on the lavender and teal hat before remembering what Mom had said. I shoved it to the back of the shelf, grabbing an older one and a pair of gloves.

"We're ready." I motioned for Cocoa, who still carried her leash in her mouth, to move to the door. Facing the two dogs now watching me from their bed, I said, "You two be good. We won't be gone long."

They plopped their heads back on their paws before I closed and locked the door. Not that I feared someone breaking in. Athena was tall enough to open doors. I didn't want her to let Lulu out. There were too many predators running around after dark not to keep a close watch on the small dog. Coyotes and owls could be heard nearly every night.

Cocoa jumped in the back seat of Rudy's pickup, and I slid into the passenger seat. As soon as he pulled onto the county road, I asked the question I'd been trying to decide if I would ask the whole time we ate pizza. "Do you know the Sheffield family?"

He glanced over at me and back at the road. "I need more than that. The name sounds familiar, but I can't place it."

"The husband came into the wool shop a couple of weeks ago to sell us black wool."

"Oh, right. Nick Sheffield and his wife, Lauren. Monica doesn't like her much." He frowned.

"How does Monica know Mrs. Sheffield?" I asked.

"They're both teachers at the high school." He glanced over at me. "Monica said that Lauren likes to fool around, if you know what I mean."

Feeling disgusted, I said, "Surely not with her students?"

"No, with the male teachers and some parents." He

shrugged. "Anyway, that's what Monica says. But she could just be jealous."

"That the other woman fools around?" I was trying to keep up with the conversation, but my mind kept going to the father and daughter who had seemed happy and loving.

"No, she doesn't want to fool around with anyone." He grinned. "Except me."

"I don't want to think about that, even if you are thirty-seven years old. You're still my little brother." I was five years older than Rudy, but there were days when I felt even older, like today.

"Sorry, too much information. Anyway, she's jealous because the principal put Lauren in for Teacher-of-the-Year over Monica. She's pretty sure Lauren gave him something for his nomination. If you know what I mean."

I stared forward as the lights of Auburn came into view. I've loved this town of 10,000 people since I was old enough to walk the streets and be greeted by the friendly community. I was born here. And now that I'm back, I don't plan on going anywhere again. My years with Mick had been full of love, excitement, and travel. Now I want to settle down and become a member of the community.

Rudy found a parking spot three blocks away from the park. We walked with other residents to the lit-up area in front of the thirty-foot-tall pine tree that had become the town's Christmas tree before I was born.

We moved through the crowd, aiming for David's unmistakable knitted cap, a good head above the rest of the crowd. Nina had gifted her husband a neon green hat with sheep parading around it several years ago.

He'd started wearing it to winter events so people could find him. As if his six-and-a-half feet didn't make him easy to find in a crowd. Mom stood beside David, but I didn't see Nina.

"Good, you two made it," Mom said, linking her arm through mine. It had been twenty-five years since I'd witnessed this event. I was excited and happy to be with my family.

"Wouldn't miss the tree lighting," I said, gazing up at the dark tree highlighted by the streetlamps behind it.

"I'm going to find Monica," Rudy said and disappeared.

"When is he going to ask that woman to marry him?" Mom asked.

"Are you ready to get rid of your roommate?" I asked.

"He might as well get married. He's not sleeping in his bed that much anyway." Mom huffed and I giggled.

"I'd know that giggle anywhere," said a voice behind me.

I spun around and stared into the unseeing eyes of my childhood friend. "Betty!" I shouted and pulled the slender, dark-skinned woman into a hug. There was no mistaking the short-cropped curls with a touch of gray, underneath a wide-brimmed hat with Christmas decorations around the crown. Even as a girl, she'd worn outlandish hats. Her mom would give her the hats, and Betty would decorate them.

Betty whispered in my ear, "I've missed you."

Leaning back, I peered under the brim of the hat. Tears glistened in her eyes. "I've missed you, too. Tell me how to get a hold of you, and we'll catch up." I looped an arm in hers as Cocoa pressed against her legs.

"Who is this?" Betty asked, her hand touching the top of Cocoa's head.

"One of my therapy dogs. Her name is Cocoa."

Betty moved her hand down Cocoa's forehead between her eyes and down her snout. "You are a beautiful creature. I can tell by how calm you are and the aura about you."

I said quietly. "You see an aura? Have you had surgery on your eyes?"

Betty smiled. "No. But I have a lot to tell you."

"Let's meet tomorrow at Bow Wow Brew, say one?" I said, wanting to find out what was up with Betty and seeing auras.

"It's a date." Betty stood beside me as the mayor appeared on the pavilion.

Mayor Tom Graham stepped up to the microphone as the town clock struck eight times. The ringing died, and the mayor raised his arms. "Welcome, everyone, to this year's tree lighting. I know how much you love to hear me talk." During the pause, everyone laughed. "Tonight, all I want to say is I hope you all have a merry Christmas and shop local. Now I'll introduce our special guest who will light the tree. Our new Sheriff, Jason Skala."

A man I had never seen before stepped up beside Tom and shook hands. He seemed young for a sheriff and looked like he could chase down criminals. The uniform wasn't distorted by a beer belly and the slacks clung to muscular legs.

The crowd stopped clapping, and the sheriff said, "Thank you, Auburn and Baker County. When I received this assignment, I was excited to get back to

Eastern Oregon. I have family not far from here and will be able to visit them more often. I look forward to keeping our county safe and getting to meet more of you." He turned to the mayor. The older man motioned for the sheriff to push the large red button beside the podium.

Sheriff Skala grinned as if he were a child opening a gift and slapped his hand down on the button.

Everyone groaned as the tree didn't light up.

Tom faced the tree and hollered, "Sheila, check the plugin."

This emitted a chuckle from the crowd. Everyone knew that Tom's wife, Sheila, was his minion.

A scream rang through the park.

The sheriff ran to the back of the pavilion and jumped down.

Cocoa pulled me away from Betty, out of the crowd, around the pavilion, and straight to Sheila, who had one hand over her mouth and the other clutching her stomach. Cocoa nudged the woman. Her hand dropped to pat the dog's head.

"What is it?" I asked her.

"What are you doing back here?" a male voice asked before Sheila pulled herself together.

I spun around and stared into the sheriff's face. "My dog dragged me back here. She heard the scream and wanted to comfort Sheila."

Sheila had dropped to her knees. She hugged Cocoa.

"This is a crime scene. You need to go over to that tree and take Sheila with you." Sheriff Skala pointed to a tree twenty feet away.

I nodded and helped Sheila to her feet. Once we

stood by the tree, I whispered, "What did you see?"

Sheila continued to pet Cocoa. "A woman with a string of lights around her neck."

I had a bad feeling. "Did you know the woman?"

Sheila nodded. "It was the teacher, Mrs. Sheffield."

Chapter Three

I thought of Ava. Had the girl told her father about seeing her mom kissing Santa? What would happen to the child if the husband had killed his wife?

"You're sure it was Mrs. Sheffield?" I asked.

"Yes. Madison had her as a teacher." Sheila didn't look up. "I'm actually surprised this hasn't happened to her sooner."

I dropped to a crouch, making the woman look at me. "What do you mean?"

"Everyone in town knows she slept with any male but her husband for the last five years."

"Meaning there are a lot of women in town who would like to kill her." I didn't envy the job the sheriff or the city police had on their hands. Many people would be willing to say the woman slept around, but I was pretty sure no one would point any fingers. This close-knit community had survived this long by banding together.

Boots appeared on the ground next to me. My gaze drifted up the length of the body. The new sheriff glared at me. I rose to my feet and then helped Sheila stand.

"Sheriff," I said.

"I've talked to City Police Chief Vern Shaw. Since I was first on the scene and have more homicide experience, I'll be heading up this investigation." His gaze shifted to Sheila. "Mrs. Graham, I'll have Deputy Harper take you to the station so we can get your statement about finding the body."

I smiled at my niece, Bailey. Nina and David had been upset when their daughter took criminal justice courses and then joined the sheriff's department, but I thought it was brave of Bailey to want to help others and step away from the sheep ranch and wool spinning.

As Bailey led Sheila away, I turned to head back to my family.

"Where are you going?" the sheriff asked, grabbing my arm.

Cocoa growled, putting herself between me and the sheriff.

He dropped his hold on my arm and studied Cocoa. "That's a protective dog you have."

"She's my protector and a therapy dog. That's why she brought me here when Sheila screamed. She wanted to help the person in distress." I patted Cocoa's smooth head. The dog had been with me the longest. Cocoa was my first therapy animal. I'd discovered the animal's desire to protect and console when I lost my husband. "All of my animals are therapy animals. They can all instinctively tell when someone needs to vent or hug something warm and loving."

The sheriff shook his head. "I've heard of therapy

animals, but most of the ones I've come across are only that by label. They don't do anything for the people that have them."

"Talk to anyone in the county. I'm sure they can tell you what these animals have done for many people. I'm at the Rockin' Retirement home every Wednesday and the hospital on Thursday afternoons. Then the different elementary schools have me come in once a quarter for the kids to take turns holding the animals. Not to mention things such as the Petting Zoo I provided today at the festival." Which flipped my thoughts to Ava and her murdered mother.

"Was whatever Sheila saw an accident?" I asked.

Sheriff Skala studied me. "What did she say she saw?"

I swallowed and ran my fingers through the thick fur on Cocoa's neck. Her fur and quiet nature had become my steadying mechanism. "She said she found a woman with a string of lights around her neck."

The sheriff shook his head. "You don't repeat whatever she said to anyone. We need to keep the information out of the public to help us with our investigation."

I nodded and found the courage to ask my next question. "Was it Mrs. Sheffield?"

"Why do you ask?" He stepped closer. A woodsy scent floated on the crisp air. I inhaled and arranged my thoughts.

"Sheila said she thought it was Mrs. Sheffield. If that's the case, you'll have a long line of people to question. I'll just get going." I tugged slightly on Cocoa's leash and she stood.

"Where are you going?"

"To find my family and go home," I said, tipping my head back slightly to peer into his eyes. It was dark enough that the brim of his hat shaded his upper face.

"I need your formal statement. You need to wait here until an officer can take it down."

"Sheriff! The M.E.s here!" called a deputy, standing over the body.

"You wait here." Sheriff Skala pointed at the ground and walked over to the deputy.

I sighed and peered out at the people in front of the pavilion. I spotted David's hat. At least my family hadn't abandoned me, and neither had most of the crowd. They had to be hanging around to find out why Sheila screamed and what brought more police and a medical examiner.

At that moment, an ambulance drove across the park and stopped only a few feet from me.

An E.M.T. slid out and walked to the back. He glanced at me and then smiled. "Hey, Andi! I hope you aren't my customer."

I recognized Bradley Brown. His daughter was one of my first therapy patients when I returned to Auburn. "Hi, Bradley. No, I'm just waiting to make a statement and go home."

He patted Cocoa's head. "Hi, Cocoa. Hannah has a dog a lot like you now. She loves that dog, and it has helped a lot with her anxiety." He glanced up at me. "I'm so glad you moved back here and knew what Hannah needed. Everyone else was going to give up on her or make her take medication."

"I'm glad we could help." I put a hand on Cocoa's head.

"Over here!" called Sheriff Skala.

"What happened?" Bradley asked as he and his partner pulled the gurney out of the back of the ambulance.

"As far as I know, Mrs. Sheffield is dead."

Bradley turned from latching the wheels down on the gurney and stared at me. "The teacher at the high school?"

"I think so. I haven't seen her, not that I'd know what she looked like, but that's what Sheila Graham said." I watched Bradley as he pushed the gurney over to the crime scene. He appeared to be deep in thought. What did he know?

"Mom sent me to see what was taking you so long." Rudy's voice came from behind me.

I spun around and put a hand on his chest, pushing him backward. "I don't think you're supposed to be here."

"Why not?" he asked loudly.

"Because this is a crime scene." Sheriff Skala strode over. "Who are you and why are you back here?"

"I'm Rudy Weber. This is my sister. Our mom sent me back here to see why she wasn't coming out so we could go home." Rudy didn't even flinch or back away as the sheriff studied him.

"I see." Sheriff Skala shifted his attention to me. "Do you have a car to get home?"

"No. I drove her here," Rudy said, becoming protective.

"You can give me the keys to your pickup and go home with Mom, Nina, and David," I said, holding my hand out.

"Why does she have to stay here any longer? Cocoa just dragged her back here when someone screamed. And why did someone scream?" Rudy was getting into the sheriff's face.

I knew this wouldn't go well. "Rudy, just hand me the keys, and the rest of you go home. Check on Athena and Lulu on the way in, please." I continued to hold my hand out, wiggling my fingers.

"Give your sister the keys. She can tell you all about it when she gets home." Sheriff Skala motioned for Rudy to hand the keys over.

Rudy dug into his pocket and dropped the keys in my hand. "Call Mom as soon as you get done with the police. You know she won't sleep until she knows you're okay."

"I will. Go." I waved him off and dropped the keys in my coat pocket.

"Is that your big brother?" the sheriff asked, taking me by the elbow and leading me toward the crime scene.

"No, my baby brother. Since I moved back to Auburn, he has been acting more like a big brother, though." I stopped, seeing how close we were getting to the person taking photos of the woman on the ground. "I don't want to go any closer." Cocoa pressed against my legs, giving me comfort.

"I just want you in the light as I ask you questions." Sheriff Skala maneuvered me to the side, where there was light from the bright beams of the floodlights that now stood around the crime scene. He settled me on the edge of the pavilion. Pulling out a notebook, he asked, "Name, occupation, and address."

"Andi, short for Andrea, Clark. I'm the bookkeeper for Weber Wool and the owner of Cuddle Farm Therapy Animals. I live at 20173 Weber Lane."

He glanced up from his notebook. "Bookkeeper for Weber Wool and you live on Weber Lane?"

"My maiden name is Weber. I live on the Weber Farm out northwest of town."

"Husband's name?"

I stared at the wedding band on my ring finger. "It was Mick. He died two years ago."

"I'm sorry for your loss. And that's when you came back to Auburn?" He studied me with dark brown eyes.

"No. I've only been back since January. It took a year to get my husband's body transported to the United States. He had an unusual job. We traveled a lot and when his death occurred, there were a lot of strings to pull and red tape to untangle."

"I see. Have you ever met Lauren Sheffield?"

"No. I only heard her name today." I didn't want to tell the sheriff about what Ava saw, but it could be a clue to who killed the woman. "Mr. Sheffield and his daughter Ava came into Weber Wool a couple weeks ago. He asked if we would buy wool from his black sheep."

The sheriff stopped writing and stared at me. "Is this a joke?"

I sputtered and then gathered my rattled mind. "No. It's not a joke. He has five head of black sheep that he wants to sell the wool from. Most big wool buyers don't like to buy black wool unless you have a whole bag. I take it you don't know anything about wool or sheep?"

"I'm a horse and cattle man myself," he said. "Continue with how you know the husband and daughter."

"Like I said, they came into the store. Then today

at the petting zoo, I said goodbye to the 4-Hers who helped me, and when I returned to the pen where my animals were, I found Ava confiding in Athena about something that had upset her."

"How can I contact Athena?" he asked.

"She's probably still curled up on her bed where I left her. She's a dog. Ava had met her on one of our trips to an elementary school. She felt comfortable telling Athena that she'd just witnessed her mom kissing Santa. And not a peck on the cheek."

Sheriff Skala stared at me. "You mean the dead woman was making out with Santa at the festival?"

"If you can believe the child. And as upset as she was, I think you can. She also said she didn't know who to tell. My guess would be she told her dad." I didn't like mentioning that, but it was the truth, and it needed to be put out there. The little bit I'd seen of Mr. Sheffield, I didn't believe he would kill his wife. But it was a huge coincidence that Ava witnessed what she did today, and tonight the woman was dead.

"I see. Was the deceased a housewife?" he asked.

"No. She was a high school teacher."

The man's gaze zinged back to my face. "A high school teacher? Chief Shaw was talking about some threats a high school teacher received when we had coffee last week." He stopped and stared at me with wide eyes as if he hadn't meant to say that out loud. "Is there anything else you want to add to your statement?"

"No. That's all I know about what might be helpful."

"You can go. But can I get your phone number in case we have follow-up questions?"

I recited my phone number and walked out through

the trees behind the pavilion to avoid the people still milling around in front. I didn't want to talk to anyone about what I knew. However, the sheriff inadvertently blurting out that the woman may have had threats against her would definitely take some of the heat off of Mr. Sheffield. I wanted the husband to be innocent for Ava's sake.

Chapter Four

As soon as I settled in Rudy's pickup with the heat going, I called Mom.

"What was that all about?" Mom asked.

"Someone was killed behind the pavilion." The sheriff hadn't told me not to reveal the victim, but I didn't want Ava or her father to hear who the victim was from anyone other than law enforcement.

"Oh, my heavens! You mean, while we were all standing there waiting for the ceremony to begin, someone was killed?"

Her comment jolted me. I hadn't thought that the woman was killed while we all stood in front of the pavilion staring up at the tree. "I don't know. I didn't see the body, and I wasn't told when the person was killed." This was all too much like the work Mick had done as we traveled around the world. He'd had top secret clearance and helped countries solve hard murder cases that dealt with the privileged and sometimes government officials. I was allowed to travel with him for cover. Not only could I keep my mouth shut, but with my accounting degree, I could work out any discrepancies to help solve money matters. My family didn't know exactly what Mick had done for work and thought I'd just been a trophy wife traveling with my husband.

"Are you home?" Mom asked.

"No. I'm warming up in Rudy's pickup while I talk to you. As soon as I hang up, I'll drive home." I studied the empty streets around me, shivered thinking about the body across the park behind the pavilion, and clicked the door lock. Auburn, even on a night when there was a ceremony at the park, was closed up. Only the two bars and one restaurant that stayed open until ten had lights on.

"Then I'll let you go so you can get home. I'll see you at work on Monday." The call ended.

I shoved my cell phone into my coat pocket and realized it was Saturday night. "We have all day to ourselves, tomorrow, Cocoa," I said, patting her head and buckling my seatbelt. I was looking forward to a leisurely day.

❁ ❁ ❁

Sunday morning, I was taking care of my usual weekend chore, cleaning out Sparky and Cupcake's indoor stalls. Lulu's sharp bark caught my attention moments before Cocoa joined in, and finally, Athena's deep 'company's coming' bark couldn't be ignored.

I walked out of the barn and spotted a pickup I didn't recognize coming down the driveway. "Lulu,

36

come!" I called the small dog that didn't know how to get out of the way of the tires and wouldn't be seen by anyone in the vehicle. Lulu came running and hopped into my arms, which were stretched down to the animal. "Who do you think that is?" I asked, petting the dog's silky black ears.

Athena had stopped barking and now wagged her baseball bat-sized tail. Cocoa trotted alongside the vehicle, sniffing.

I recognized Sheriff Skala as he stepped out of the unmarked vehicle in his uniform.

Walking toward the man, I had the distinct feeling he was sizing up my place and the animals. "Did you have more questions?" I asked, stopping ten feet from him.

"Yeah, and I wanted to see Athena since she was the animal you heard the girl talking to." He reached out and scratched Lulu's ears. "Is this Athena?"

I smiled indulgently and shook my head. "No, Athena is the monster beating you with her tail."

Sheriff Skala dropped his hand and patted Athena on the head. "Wow, I can't imagine too many kids would cuddle up to a dog this size."

"She actually has more kids wanting to visit with her than Lulu. I think because she's kind of like a big stuffed animal to them." I nodded to the house. "Want some coffee or hot chocolate while we talk?"

"Sounds good. I didn't make it to bed last night."

The phrase, the setting, him, the animals, it all felt like something I'd experienced before. The word for it is déjà vu. I stutter-stepped as the whole thing made me wonder why I'd have this moment.

In the kitchen, I set out muffins I'd made that

morning and poured the sheriff a cup of coffee. We settled at the kitchen table, and Sheriff Skala peeled the wrapper off a muffin.

"How did Mr. Sheffield and his daughter take the news?" I asked, holding a cup of coffee between my hands and watching him.

He put the muffin down and peered into my eyes. "Like anyone who was awakened from sleep and told their loved one was dead." He shook his head. "They both took it poorly. I don't think he killed her. But I can't rule him out. Spouses are usually the killers. According to him and Ava, they went to the tree lighting because Mrs. Sheffield was already there setting up. The husband didn't know much about his wife's movements. Only that she was on the festival and tree lighting committee. When the tree didn't light, he took his daughter home, figuring his wife would be busy working with the other committee members to figure out what went wrong and reschedule the lighting."

I could imagine the shock and hurt the two were going through. "Did he say where he was before the lighting? Or at the time of death?"

The sheriff's gaze remained on my face. "Why are you asking these questions? Do you know something you haven't told us?"

"No. I told you everything. I'm just wondering if she was killed while we were all standing there waiting or if it happened earlier." I'd thought about the timing last night after Mom's comment. I'd also contemplated if the man I saw after the festival should be mentioned.

"We're waiting for the autopsy report. But she'd been there long enough for her body to cool."

I ran a finger around the rim of my coffee cup, stalling to make up my mind.

"Spit out whatever it is you think you need to say." Sheriff Skala picked up his coffee and drank, watching me over the rim.

"I was leaving the festival yesterday as the sun was going down. The man who had dressed up as Santa walked away from the area with an angry expression and long strides." I held his gaze. "I don't know if he might be the killer or not, but given what Ava saw and then her mom ending up dead…"

"What's his name?" Sheriff Skala picked up his pen.

"I don't know. You'd have to ask the chair of the festival committee. I think that was Sheila Graham." I wondered how the mayor's wife was holding up this morning. She'd had quite a shock the night before.

"I have Deputy Harper rounding up the names of all the people who had booths at the event yesterday. And a map to see which booths were close to the crime scene." He plucked another muffin from the plate in the middle of the table.

"She's very reliable," I said with a smile.

"You know Deputy Harper?"

"She's my niece. My older sister's daughter. I was happy when she said she wanted to be in law enforcement. She actually broke away from the line of women who spin, knit, and weave wool in this family." I shrugged. "I did too. At least the spinning, knitting, and weaving. I'm still working for the family business, just not playing with wool."

"Why don't you play with wool?" he asked, taking a bite.

"I'm not creative that way. I prefer playing with animals and crunching numbers. I went to college to become an accountant."

He watched me with interest. There was something about the man that made me feel comfortable. I decided to tell him more about me.

"Then I married and traveled the world using my accounting to help my husband with his job." I smiled. We had been to some beautiful places and some scary places, but I always knew that Mick would keep me safe. If only he'd been more observant the day he was hit while crossing a street in Dublin. We'd gone there on vacation. He had wanted to go to a country we hadn't seen yet.

"What was your husband's job?"

The sheriff's voice brought me back from my reminiscing. I smiled and said, "He was an investment banker for foreign countries." I watched the man sitting across from me. He still seemed genuinely interested in what I was saying. I toyed with telling him about Mick's real job, but refrained. I had kept the secret for 20 years; I could keep it longer.

"How did your husband die? Heart attack?" the sheriff asked.

"We were on vacation in Dublin. He went out to get us more wine. He didn't return when he should have, and an hour later, I had a garda show up asking if I knew a Mick Clark." The loss struck me again. The day flooded my mind. I felt as if I staggered back into the chair just as I had when the garda told me he was dead. I couldn't talk for the lump of sorrow in my throat.

"I'm sorry I brought up a bad memory." Sheriff

Skala slid my cup of coffee closer, then reached across the table and put a hand on mine.

I swallowed several times, getting my emotions under control. I could be stoic when people didn't get mushy, but his trying to console me brought up the grief I'd been working to overcome. Drawing my hand out from under his, I picked up the coffee cup and said, "Thank you." After several sips, my throat seemed to work again. I continued, "I'm slowly getting used to living each day without him."

Sheriff Skala nodded. "I know the feeling. I lost my wife ten years ago."

"I'm sorry to hear that. Do you have any advice for someone who recently lost the love of their life?" I felt my wayward strands of gray hair tickling my forehead. The coarse stragglers popped out all the time, giving my auburn hair a tinsel look. I shoved them off my forehead, waiting for him to gather the words.

He blew out a breath and said, "Just keep waking up each day and know that your spouse would want you to move on with your life." His gaze locked onto mine. "That and I have a son, who reminds me every day of the joys my wife and I had before she died." He nodded toward my dogs. "You have them to get you out of bed every day. That's moving forward."

I hadn't planned on getting a therapy session from him. "Can we focus on Mrs. Sheffield, please?" I knew that sounded rude, considering I was the one who'd asked for his advice.

"I think I've gathered all I need from you. For now." The sheriff stood. "Thanks for the coffee and muffins. That should get me through until I can call it a day and take a few hours off."

"I thought there was a detective on the county staff," I said, remembering something I'd read in the paper about the detective discovering a theft ring.

"He's on vacation. Went skiing with his family for two weeks. I'm the lead until he gets back. In a small community like this, the sooner we catch the killer, the sooner things will get back to normal."

I agreed with that. Walking the sheriff out to his vehicle, I decided to call Sheila and see how she was holding up. And maybe see who had been the Santa at the festival.

Chapter Five

"Andi, I'm so glad you called. I felt bad that I wasn't more coherent last night when we were talking," Sheila said after I had told her I was calling to check up on her.

"It's understandable. It's not every day that a person finds someone dead." I planned to get the information about the Santa from Sheila, but the conversation took a twist.

"You know, the last body I found was my mother. Dead in her bed when I went to visit her last year. No one had checked on her, and I'd tried calling for two days without her answering the phone. I'd expected to find out she'd fallen and a neighbor had picked her up and taken her to a hospital. But no. I unlocked the door and walked in, calling for her. I could tell something was wrong by the smell." She made a sound in her throat. "It was horrid. I found Mom sitting up in bed, a book on her lap, her eyes wide open. Startled me. Then

I figured out she was dead and called her doctor and the mortuary.”

“I’m sorry you had to go through that, Sheila.” I paused briefly and asked, “I was wondering what exactly Mrs. Sheffield’s duties were on the festival and tree lighting committee?”

“What do you mean?” Sheila sounded surprised.

“Her husband said she was on the committee. I just wanted to know what her duties were.”

“Oh no. She wasn’t on the committee. But she did come to me and say she had a volunteer to be Santa.”

I found a piece of paper and jotted down, *Not on the committee*. “What was the volunteer’s name?”

“She didn’t give me a name. Lauren insisted that she would get him all the information and make sure he showed up.” There was a pause. “But I think he was one of her lovers.”

I stared at the cell phone and asked, “One of her lovers? As in she had more than one at a time?” This would make for a lot more suspects for the sheriff to interview.

“That’s the gossip going around the sewing circle and book club. And her husband is so nice. I can’t believe a woman would cheat on him. That little girl of theirs is darling, too.”

“Did her husband know she was cheating?” That would definitely be a reason for him to want to get rid of his wife and keep his daughter.

“I don’t think he did, even though everyone else in the county knew. He stays to himself on the farm and only comes to town for his daughter’s school events. I think Lauren liked it that way. She could have her men and not let her husband get wind of it.”

"But if she was that disheartened by her marriage, why didn't she just divorce her husband?" I never understood a woman who stayed in an unhappy marriage when it was so easy to get divorced. I had an acquaintance in Milan who had complained so much about her husband that I told her to get a divorce. She adamantly backtracked, saying she loved him, she just didn't care for some of the things he did. Yet the woman seemed genuinely unhappy.

"I think she liked the thrill of playing the field and keeping it from her husband. And she liked getting the wives of the men she fooled around with upset. It was as if she thrived on making the other women unhappy or angry."

"You mean she didn't even try to keep her lovers secret?" I wrote down: *Killer could be any wife in town.* Then added *or husband.*

"Oh no! She has nearly ruined at least half a dozen marriages that I know of because she would gloat to the wife and then dump the husband. Honestly, someone did this town a favor. But don't tell the police I said that."

I finished by asking if they knew when the tree lighting would be rescheduled and discovered they had postponed it until the following Saturday. "That's probably a good idea. Who knows how long the police will need to look for evidence in that area."

"I hadn't thought of that. We thought Saturday night was best so the children could attend." Sheila said something away from the phone and then said, "I have to go. Sheriff Skala just stopped by."

Silence on the other end of the call. The sheriff must have driven straight from here to Sheila's. Before

I could get my boots on to go back to the barn, someone banged through my front door.

"Who's there?" I called out.

"It's us." Rudy appeared, followed by Mom and Nina.

"What brings all of you to my house?" I kicked off the one boot I had on and walked into the kitchen to pour them all a cup of coffee.

They were all seated at my small kitchen table when I handed out full mugs.

"We saw the sheriff visited you. Are you a suspect?" Mom asked.

I laughed. "No, I'm not a suspect. He just wanted to ask me a few more questions. And I asked him some as well."

"We heard who died. And you were asking me about the family as we drove into town last night," Rudy said, raising his cup to his lips. "Makes me wonder what you know about the family."

"As much as you told me. Which sounds like the police will have a lot of suspects." I brought the cup to my lips and sipped, watching everyone over the rim. Each one had multiple ways of knowing everything about the Sheffield family and possible suspects.

"You didn't tell the sheriff how Monica was upset about not getting the nomination for Teacher of the Year, did you?" Rudy asked.

"No. I'm sure Lauren Sheffield was killed by someone other than Monica." I glanced at Mom. She was staring into her coffee. "What do you know about Lauren, Mom?"

Mom's head jerked up as she peered into my eyes. "More than I care to know, and I agree, there will be a long list of suspects."

"Who were her most recent lovers?" I asked.

Mom flinched at the use of the word. "Why do you want to know?" she asked.

"I'm curious. I like Ava and I don't want to see her hurt by this dragging out if I can help find the killer." I knew a bit about following clues and digging for dirt from helping Mick. My family didn't know that, but I didn't see why I couldn't use some of what he taught me to help the community find a killer.

"What makes you think you can find the killer?" Nina asked, her tone half curious but in her accusatory timbre that always grated on my nerves.

"Because of some things I saw and information I'll gather." I shifted my gaze and attention to Mom. "Do you happen to know who the Santa was yesterday?"

"I only caught a glimpse of him when I used the restroom. I thought his voice sounded like Kyle Stevens, one of the real estate agents in town. Why?" Mom stared at me.

"He was hand-picked by Lauren."

Nina snorted and said, "You think Lauren was having an affair with Kyle? There's no way. He's married to Viola."

"Viola? Your best friend?" I didn't like that I would have to deal with not only the Homecoming Queen and head cheerleader but also Nina if I found out that Viola could have killed Lauren.

"Yes. Viola and Kyle have been together since high school and they are both deeply in love with each other. You can see it when you watch them together. Kyle would never do anything to hurt Viola." Nina crossed her arms and glared at me.

"Who usually dressed up as Santa for the festival?" I asked. I was sure the man who had when I was a child was no longer alive.

"Last year, it was Waldo Dennis, the principal at the high school. Before that, it was Tom Graham until he became mayor and thought it was unfitting for him to be Santa," Mom said.

I shifted and studied Rudy. "You said Monica thought Lauren had given the principal a favor to get his nomination. Why would she take his Santa gig away from him if she was trying to make nice with him?"

Rudy shrugged.

"Is the principal married?" I asked.

"Widower. His wife died four years ago," Mom said.

I had an idea that the principal may have been trying to win Lauren's favor, and not the other way around.

"I need to go see some people." I rose from the table, put my mug in the sink, and called the dogs. "Come on, let's go for a drive."

"Where are you going?" Mom asked as she gathered Rudy and Nina's cups with hers and stood.

"I'll walk the dogs in the park, visit with Betty, and see if I can get a handle on the gossip going around town."

Nina snorted and said, "Betty? Blind Betty? Why would you want to talk to her? Rumor is she's going crazy, talking about auras when we all know she can't see anything."

Nina has always been mean to Betty. She and Viola had played jokes on me and Betty all through school. Their cruelty was one of the many things that made us friends.

"Betty is a friend, and I've been neglecting my friends. It's time to start reconnecting." I picked up Lulu and the other two dogs followed me to the van. After putting their harnesses on and clipping them to the seatbelt, I climbed into the driver's seat and watched Mom and my siblings walk up the driveway to their respective houses.

Chapter Six

In town, I went straight to the park. There was still one county vehicle parked as close to the pavilion as it could get without being on the grass. It was noon. People were milling about on the streets, coming from church or just getting up and heading out for lunch. Only the chain stores, restaurants, coffee shops, and gas stations were open on Sunday.

I parked around the corner from the county car and stepped out. Sliding the van door open, I unhooked the dogs and clipped on their leashes.

"Let's go for a walk in the park this morning," I said, closing and locking the van door. I dropped the van keys in the fanny pack I'd buckled on. It held dog treats, doggy poop bags, and my wallet.

I followed the trio of dogs around to several trees. They sniffed up the trunks, no doubt following the scent of squirrels. While they sniffed, I craned my neck to see if I knew the deputy watching the crime scene.

My phone dinged from the depths of my fanny pack. I dug it out and smiled. A text message from Bailey.

I see you trying not to snoop. Come on over.

I was in luck. I did know the deputy on duty. I slipped the phone back in my little pack. "Come on, girls, let's go see Bailey."

Walking across the park toward the back of the pavilion, Bailey walked out and met me. "I can't have your dogs walking all over the crime scene."

"That's fine. I don't really want to see it. I was just hoping to learn a little bit."

Bailey cocked her head much like Cocoa did when she was curious about a sound she'd heard. "Why do you want to learn something?"

"I like Ava, the victim's daughter. I want to help her get closure."

"I'd think just letting her visit with your animals would be enough for you to do." Bailey stood with her arms crossed, her feet spread wide, like she was trying to bar me from more than just the scene.

"My animals will be available to her, but I just feel like I have the clue to this, but can't figure it out." I peered at my niece. "Do you understand what I'm saying?"

Bailey held eye contact and nodded her head. "I've had that a time or two before I became a deputy, and after."

"Something someone said or did is the clue to who killed Lauren. But I can't put my finger on what it is." I didn't usually try to sway someone, especially my niece, with a misdirection of information, but in this case… "Sheriff Skala came by this morning to pick my brain some more. I think that's what really set off my inner niggling that I should know something."

Bailey dropped her crossed arms and stared at me. "Really? The sheriff came to you for help?"

"Not help, just coffee, muffins, and he asked me a few more questions."

"He's not anything like Sheriff Wayne. Word is, he applied for this job to be closer to his family on the Umatilla Reservation." Bailey nodded her head.

"I'm glad he's able to be closer to family. That's why I moved back here." Losing my husband and growing older, I had been drawn back to Auburn with a deep desire to connect with my family and community again. Traveling and meeting so many interesting people was fun with Mick. Once he was gone, I felt out of place in foreign countries and yearned to get back to my roots.

"Have you learned anything about the time of death?" I asked.

Cocoa and Lulu both woofed. I glanced in the direction they were both looking and cringed inside.

Sheriff Skala strode across the park toward us. When he stopped to the side of us, Athena tugged on her leash and walked over to him, raising her head for a pet. He dropped his hand and stroked her head. "What are you doing here Ms. Clark?" he asked.

"Please, call me Andi. Ms. Clark sounds like I should be walking around in high heels and short skirts."

His eyes lit up briefly before he turned his attention to Bailey. "What are you doing talking to a civilian?"

"She's my aunt. We were discussing family." She

shrugged and gave me a look that said don't get me in trouble.

He shifted his gaze back to me. "I'm surprised to see you in town. The last time I saw you, you were cleaning out stalls."

"Ever since you asked me questions this morning, I've had this faint niggling in my head that I know something, but I can't get it to come to the surface. I thought maybe being back here would jog it loose."

"Did it?" he asked, continuing to study me.

"Nope. I do have some names you might want to talk to. Since you're new in town, the locals aren't going to open up to you and spill all the gossip, like I was hit with this morning after you left."

"That's true, sir," Bailey added. "Just this morning, when I was getting a coffee, Mollie Tweedie, at the coffee shop, told me she saw Lauren in the coffee shop two days ago with Kyle Stevens. Who also dressed as Santa yesterday."

I couldn't believe Bailey was telling the sheriff about her mom's best friend's husband. It was different if it came from me. Viola and I hadn't been on friendly terms since I started school. The woman was too worried about her status in the town rather than how she could help the community.

Sheriff Skala pulled out his notebook and asked, "You said, Mollie Tweedie?"

Bailey nodded when the sheriff looked up at her.

"Where does she work?"

Bailey glanced at me and rolled her eyes, then said, "The only coffee shop open early on Sunday. *Better Brew*."

The sheriff glared at his deputy and said, "I've only

been here three weeks and haven't learned all the businesses and what days they are open. Your job is to help me learn all of this, not make fun of me. Is that clear?"

"Yes, sir," Bailey's face paled at the reprimand.

I decided to take the heat off my niece. "Bailey's worked hard to be in law enforcement. I won't do anything to sully her reputation as a deputy."

Sheriff Skala nodded. "I know about her accomplishments. I checked out all the deputies before I signed on for this job."

"Then you know you are working with good people. I'm off to meet a friend." I made a kissy sound, and all three dogs stood and started walking ahead of me.

"Wait up!" Sheriff Skala called.

I stopped and glanced at him over my shoulder.

He jogged up beside me. "You need to keep your nose out of this. Sheila Graham told me you called her this morning."

"To see how she was doing. She didn't look well last night." I wasn't going to let him keep me from finding the truth for Ava.

"I know you think I won't be able to get answers because I'm new. My deputies have been here most of them their whole lives. I'm sure working with them, we'll learn all we need to know. Stay away from this homicide. You could get yourself or someone you love hurt by digging around."

Shaking my head, I said, "I'm not going to put myself in danger. I only want to help you find the truth."

"We don't need your help. We'll get to the truth."

He scowled and patted Athena's head.

"To get the truth quicker, you'll need to rely on Bailey, and whoever else has lived here a long time, who you trust. Believe me. I grew up here. I know how the locals close ranks to keep friends and family safe." I faced the street and started walking.

He caught up to me. "I get your point. I grew up on the Umatilla Reservation. I understand being wary of outsiders. But my deputies will ask the questions, not you."

"Fine." I was done talking to the man. It was clear he planned to solve his first homicide in Auburn all by himself. All I could think was, if he only knew the skills Mick taught me. But I wasn't ready to reveal my former life, if ever.

"If you're through telling me to butt out, I'm meeting someone at the Bow Wow Brew in fifteen minutes." I glanced from him to the coffee shop across the street and back to him.

"Are we clear on you staying out of my investigation?" he asked.

"Crystal," I said, looking both ways and then crossing the street with my three dogs leading the way.

Chapter Seven

On the opposite corner sat Bow Wow Brew, a coffee shop that sold sandwiches and had a covered patio where people and their dogs could sit and eat. They even made dog cookies and had several water bowls set out. At this time of the year, the patio had propane heaters and heated water bowls. The proprietors realized dogs needed to be walked all year round and their owners would stop in where it was warm before heading home.

I found a corner table and placed Lulu on a chair, wrapping her leash around the back, and told the other two dogs to sit and stay. Not seeing Betty outside, I entered the small shop. Sitting under a Thanksgiving-themed hat was Betty.

"Betty, I'm here." I put a hand on her shoulder.

"I'm early. I wanted to save us a seat," Betty said, smiling.

"I appreciate your thoughtfulness, but we need to sit outside, if you don't mind. I have my dogs with me."

I put a hand on her elbow, as I'd been taught to do by her mother. As I directed her out of the shop, I called out to the barista to bring Betty's drink outside. She nodded, and we exited the small building to sit out under the heaters scattered around the covered outdoor seating.

"How many dogs do you have?" Betty asked, feeling the bench and sitting.

"Three. You met Cocoa, my brown and white border collie, last night. Today I also have Athena," I patted the bench beside Betty. Athena placed her head there. "You can pet her head on the left side of the bench."

Betty slowly lowered her hand and touched the top of Athena's head. "Oh! She's a big one! But so sweet. She has a blue aura. This one will protect and support you."

"She does. How do you see an aura?" I asked, feeling as awestruck by Betty's words as I'd been when we were children and she could hear something that I couldn't.

"It's not something I want to go into today. This is about catching up." Betty continued to pet Athena's head. "You have someone else with you."

"Yes. Lulu." I unhooked her leash and set her on Betty's lap.

"Oh my! Such a little body and such a big heart!" Betty held Lulu with one hand and smoothed the soft hair of the dog's ears with her other hand.

"Do you want to hold her while I place my order?" I asked, feeling good about the smile on my friend's lips and the glint in her eyes.

"I would be pleased to sit with these three." Cocoa

had pressed up against Betty's right leg.

"I'll be right back."

The barista put a drink on the counter as I walked up. "This is for Betty."

"Thanks. I need to order two dog cookies, a turkey sandwich, and a hot chocolate, please." I paid and carried Betty's drink back to her. It smelled earthy.

"Here's your drink," I said, placing the cup on the table directly in front of her.

Betty raised her right hand and found the cup. She raised it to her lips, drank, and smiled. "They make the best matcha tea in all of Baker County."

"I have been stopping in here nearly every day since I've been back. How is it we haven't bumped into one another?" I asked.

Betty's expression saddened. "I've only been back home about a month. My father passed away five years ago, and my mother last winter."

I put my hand on her arm. "I'm sorry to hear that. Your mom was so good at helping us navigate the harshness of being different in this community."

Betty spit out the tea she had in her mouth, wiped her lips with a napkin, and said, "You weren't different. I was blind and black."

"Oh, I was. I hung out with the smart girls. Nerds, we were called. And then, because I was your friend, I received a lot of torment. But it didn't matter. I knew we were friends." I grasped her hand. "We still are." This was the first time since Mick's death that I felt like I had someone I could confide in.

"I've missed you," Betty said. "Anyway, after Mom passed, I found information in her stuff about my adoption and where I came from in Ethiopia. I hired someone to take me there and try to find my village, but after two months of nothing, I realized the person I hired was taking advantage of my blindness. I fired her and found the ministry where my parents worked when they adopted me." She sipped her tea and sighed. "I'm not sure what I was hoping to find, but when I finally found a relative, all they did was ask me if I had money, did I make a lot of money, could I spare some for them. They didn't ask about my life, say they missed me, or had hoped to find me one day. It wasn't at all what I had hoped for when I set out to find my relatives."

"I'm sorry." I rose to put an arm around her shoulders when my name was called. "I'll be right back, that's our lunch." I walked over, picked up the tray, and headed back to the table.

The dogs knew the routine. Lulu jumped back in her chair and waited impatiently as I unwrapped a cookie. I broke off a third of it, handing it to her. The rest of it, Cocoa took gingerly from my hand. Then I unwrapped the other cookie and gave it to Athena. The three were busy eating their cookies as I unwrapped my sandwich.

"They sound like they are enjoying whatever you gave them," Betty said.

"Dog cookies. That's why they behave so well. They know they will get a treat." I sipped my hot chocolate and asked, "What have you been doing for work? Do you make enough that you can send money to your family in Ethiopia?"

Betty shook her head. "I don't plan to send money to them. I realize they would not use it well. I received schooling on computers, and I am a software developer for the vision-impaired. I work from home and have made a good living. It's how I paid for Mom to be in assisted living the last year after her stroke. I couldn't take care of her and help pay the bills."

"You've had to deal with so much all alone." My heart went out to my friend. "I wish I had known what you were dealing with. I would have come home sooner, and it might have brought me out of my grief sooner."

She put a hand on mine. "I heard you lost your husband. I'm sorry. Your mom told me what a wonderful couple you were and how she was proud of your courage to travel around the world."

"Really? She said that? She always said she was proud of me, but didn't say why. I thought it was because I'd found a good man and was able to help support us with my accounting." I chastised myself for fibbing a bit. My money wasn't anything compared to what Mick was paid for his services. Luckily, he'd tucked half of every job away for our retirement. I hadn't told my family, but I was a rich woman. His insurance had paid for the house and barn I built.

"You're giving off an aura that tells me you have secrets." Betty set her cup down. "Are they secrets you'll tell me?"

I studied my friend. She would never tell anyone, and I needed a confidante if I planned to discover who killed Ava's mom. "This is just between you and me. My family doesn't even know."

Betty leaned over the table toward me. She held up a hand with her pinky finger extended. "Pinky swear."

I linked my pinky with hers just as we'd done hundreds of times as children. She shook and then I leaned over the table and whispered to her what I'd been withholding from everyone else.

She leaned back, a smile curved her lips, and she said, "That is so you! Why are you keeping it to yourself?"

"Between you and me. I'm not sure my husband's death was an accident. I think someone might have found out what he did and taken revenge." I glanced around. "And I want to prove to this new sheriff that I can help him solve his homicide. I helped Mick enough that I should be able to figure this out."

Betty straightened and said, "I can be your sidekick. What can I do to help?"

Two other dog owners entered the patio area. One had a large rottweiler cross, and the other had a shaggy dog of unknown breed. I didn't know either of the people.

"Here's what I know so far." I brought her up to date on what people had to say about the deceased, what I saw at the festival and the tree lighting, and my feelings about Ava and wanting to find the truth for the child.

"I can see where you would be torn with one of your suspects being Viola's husband. That woman hasn't changed since school. She's as vindictive and mean as she ever was. Why your sister hangs out with her, I don't know. Viola has a black and brown aura. She is full of anger, greed, and self-absorption. Nina has a lemon-yellow and black. The black in her signifies suffering from something in the past, and the yellow is fear of loss. Perhaps losing something she can't control. I've often wondered why Nina, with her creative mind and yet being so sensitive, could tolerate Viola."

"I've wondered that for years and never understood it." I finished my sandwich as I watched the clientele going in and out of the shop. Many of the people I remembered from before I moved away.

Jessica Malone, well, that was her name when we went to school, I didn't know if she was married or not, came out of the shop and walked by the entrance to the patio. She glanced in, then stopped, and smiled. "Andi! I heard you were back." She detoured into the patio.

"Hi, Betty, it's Jessica. I heard about your mom, I'm sorry," she said, sitting down across from my dogs and between Betty and I.

"Thank you," Betty said, her hands stilling on her cup.

"Are these part of your therapy animals?" Jessica asked.

"Yes." I patted each dog on the head and said their names. "I also have a pygmy goat, mini donkey, rabbit, and silky chicken." I was proud of my menagerie of animals, who helped so many with anxiety, depression, and grief.

"I've heard good things about the work you do. My Lizzie talked about the day you brought the animals to Sanger Elementary for weeks afterward. Your animals make an impression on those you help."

Pride warmed my chest. "Thank you. I know Cocoa helped me during a tough time in my life, and I've strived to find other animals with the right instincts to help people who need extra silent help." I patted Cocoa's head and then Athena's and Lulu's. All of my pets could tell when someone needed their company.

Jessica's smile dimmed and she nodded. "I heard you lost your husband. I wish I'd had a chance to meet him."

That's when I realized how cut off from my past life I'd been while traveling around the world with Mick. I'd lost track of my school friends and even my cousins. I'd only stayed in contact with my immediate family because they wouldn't allow me to forget about them.

"You would have liked him. He was quick-witted and got along with everyone he came in contact with. But his job kept us moving all the time." At the time, I'd love the new experiences and the excitement of his next job. Now, I only wanted to plant my feet and never leave Baker County.

"Yes, your mom said you were traveling all over the world for his job. What did he do? She never could really tell me. And you? Did you work?" Jessica had been one of the girls I had connected with in high school. There had been five of us who had excelled at math and science. The boys thought we had cooties because we were smarter than they were, but we knew that one day, they would be working for us. At least that's what we plotted while hanging out together.

"Mick was a financial investment analyst for foreign countries. I used my accounting degree to help him crunch numbers. We had our own company, just the two of us, and traveled where we were asked for help." I'd lain awake nights after Mick died, figuring out how to describe to people a reasonable explanation of his and my work. This was the best I could come up with. I glanced at Betty. She had a slight smile. She knew the truth, and I could tell it made her happy.

Jessica smiled and nodded her head.

I must have made it sound plausible.

"Good. I was afraid you'd not used that brain of yours. I'll never forget when you answered that math question in algebra before anyone else had even written down the equation. I was so proud of you that day."

My cheeks heated at her compliment. "Thanks, I was pretty proud of myself when Mr. Shock said I was correct. I'd pushed the equation around in my head so fast, I wasn't sure I'd figured it out correctly."

Jessica chuckled. "Tiff is still around. The three of us should get together for a girls' night."

"That sounds like fun. What about Emily and Sarah?" I was curious about what the rest of the Smart Girls Club were doing after all these years. It had been a long time since I'd even thought of them. But seeing Jessica brought back fond memories.

"Emily is a doctor in Portland, and Sarah works for a drug research company. They both went the medical route. I took accounting and keep books for many businesses in town, and Tiff is running her family's ranch." Jessica stood. "I need to go, I'm sure my family is wondering what took me so long to get my caffeine fix. It was good seeing both of you, and I'll definitely give you a call."

"Same." I watched Jessica walk away and glanced at Betty. Why had I been back for ten months and not contacted any of my friends? Mom would probably say I was slowly getting back into the routine of my old life. But I felt like it was because after living in foreign countries and being an outsider for twenty years, I had learned not to seek friendships. And with the work Mick and I did, we couldn't afford to have anyone discover our true job.

"It's okay. We all understand you are working your

way back into living in a small town," Betty said.

I glanced at my unseeing friend and realized she saw more than those of us with sight. "Thank you. I need to give myself more slack."

"Yes, you do. You've had some big changes in a short amount of time. Give yourself time to heal and settle." Betty put her hand out.

I set a hand in hers, and she squeezed.

"Keep your ears open and let me know if you hear anything about the victim." I stood, gathering up the leashes and then the garbage on the table.

"Give me your phone number." Betty held her phone out to me. I added my contact information to her phone.

"I'll let you know if I hear anything," Betty said, standing and using her colorful ribbon-wrapped cane to find her way out onto the street.

I walked the dogs to the garbage can, deposited our trash, and then left the patio. On the walk back to the van, I reflected on how Auburn hadn't changed, but I had. I saw things differently now and appreciated the small community and unhurried life more.

Chapter Eight

Back home, I donned my muck boots and headed to the barn to finish cleaning out the stalls. I'd finished Sparky's that morning before Sheriff Skala arrived. Now I needed to clean up Cupcake's. While the two animals got along, I felt it was good to let them have their own space, but next to one another so they wouldn't feel lonely.

While I cleaned Cupcake's pen, I put her in with Sparky. Wheeling the last wheelbarrow load to the manure and straw pile, I spotted Mom turning her Mini Cooper into my driveway. I wanted to finish my task, so I wheeled the empty wheelbarrow back to the barn and tossed hay into the pen.

"You saw me, why did you make me walk through the mud to get here?" she asked.

"Because I've had enough interruptions today and wanted to get this finished before I had another one." I straightened and studied Mom. She was dressed as if she were headed to a dinner. "Where are you going?" I walked over and opened Sparky's pen to get Cupcake.

"I made dinner plans with Brenda. Do you want to go along, or will I have to remember what she tells me?" Mom backed up as I held onto the baling twine I'd just put around Cupcake's neck to lead her over to her open gate.

"Brenda Warren? She's still alive?"

"What do you mean, still alive? We were in school together." Mom's face reddened, and her drawn-on eyebrows formed an arch over her narrowed eyes behind bejeweled glasses.

"Sorry! She just always felt like an old woman to me. I don't think I've run across her since I've been back." I latched the gate and asked. "How long do I have to get ready?"

Mom scrutinized the Fitbit on her wrist and said, "Fifteen minutes."

"Then you'll have to feed the dogs, while I take a shower and dress." I headed to the house with Mom and the dogs on my heels.

Mom or Rudy cared for my animals when I had to take one of them to be certified as a therapy animal, or when I traveled to take a class on training therapy animals.

In the house, I said, "Cocoa, Athena, Lulu, behave," and headed to my bedroom and the shower.

❀ ❀ ❀

Sitting in the spacious and noisy dining room of the oldest and most prestigious restaurant in town, I wondered who had picked the restaurant—Mom or

Brenda. The old oak walls had the perfect patina of years of polishing, and the tables and chairs fit the opulent ambiance of the building.

"Brenda, do you remember Andi, my youngest daughter?" Mom asked as we sat at a table already occupied by the woman I'd always thought of as the witch of Auburn. Not because she had a crooked nose, a wart, or a cackle. But because she always seemed to know everything about everyone. I thought she must have magic or a crystal ball.

"Andrea, how nice to see you again," Brenda said, stretching out a thin, long hand with bracelets dangling from her wrist.

"Mrs. Warren," I said, shaking hands.

"Please, you're old enough now to call me Brenda. I'm pleased your mother brought you along. I'm interested in these animals of yours that so many people have been talking about." Brenda picked up her glass of something amber with ice and sipped.

The table was round but small enough that we could talk, and our voices wouldn't carry to the next table. Instead, they would be drowned out by the other noises around us. I picked up the menu, winced at the prices on most of the food, and settled for an Asian salad. When I put the menu back down, Brenda was staring at me. If I hadn't traveled the world and met all kinds of intimidating people, I might have shrank in my seat, thinking she was trying to read everything I ever did wrong in my mind.

The waitress arrived to take our orders. After ordering, Brenda said, "Tell me what it was you and your husband did while traveling around the world?"

I told her the same thing I'd told Jessica earlier that

day.

Brenda nodded. "It's nice to have clarification. Your mother never seemed to know how to explain it." She gave Mom a disapproving stare.

"Probably because I didn't give her a good enough explanation," I said, taking the heat off Mom.

"What do you think of Lauren Sheffield's death?" Mom asked, cutting right to the reason for the dinner.

"I could have told you that woman would come to a bad end. The way she slept with men and then flaunted it in the faces of their wives. I wonder it hadn't happened sooner." Brenda picked up her drink and downed the remaining quarter of a glass.

The waitress returned to refill Brenda's glass and see if our waters needed to be topped off.

"Of those wives, who would you put on a list of possible suspects?" I asked.

"Viola Stevens, Tilly MacDonald, Janet Bowen, and Sheila Graham." Brenda winked. "Those are the ones who try too hard to make others think their marriages are perfect."

I didn't know Tilly and Janet, but I did know Viola and Sheila. And Sheila found the body. "Is there any other reason you'd pick them over the others you know of?" From what everyone was saying, I had expected her to name off a dozen wronged women whom I could whittle away at. Not my sister's best friend and the mayor's wife.

"Viola, because she prides herself on being perfect. With Kyle straying towards Lauren, he made her look not so perfect."

"But wouldn't she take that out on Kyle and not Lauren?" I asked, thinking the man was as much to blame as Lauren. He was the one who took her up on her offer.

"Oh, I'm sure she has, she just wouldn't let anyone else see it." Brenda nodded and downed more of her drink.

Our meals arrived, and I dug into my salad trying to figure out how to approach Viola and not make Nina mad at me for the rest of our lives.

"Are you sure that Tom was one of Lauren's trophies?" Mom asked Brenda as she cut into the chicken breast, smothered in mushroom gravy, on her plate.

"I'm still wondering about that, but Sheila believes he was. Sheila thinks that Tom gave the job of finding the Santa for the festivities to Lauren because they were fooling around." Brenda picked up her four-inch-tall burger and shoved it into her mouth.

"I was told that Waldo Dennis, the principal, usually dressed up as Santa. I think Lauren put herself in charge of getting a new Santa to get back at him." I watched Brenda. Her eyes began to twinkle.

Brenda put down the burger, wiped her mouth, and said, "I can see her doing that. I'd heard and seen Waldo acting like a teenager around Lauren. He had it bad for her, and she didn't want anything to do with him. He was a widower and nothing to make a scandal out of. Other than her being married, which she seemed to conveniently forget."

Which brought me to my next question. "Do you think Nick Sheffield knew about his wife sleeping with just about all the men in Auburn?" I picked up my water and sipped as I watched Brenda.

She picked up her burger, peered at me over the

bun, and said, "There is no way he didn't know what his wife was doing. And that cute little girl of theirs knew. Children hear everything that goes on between their parents. I'm sure a couple of the kids at school told her about her mom causing trouble. And she would have heard her own parents quarreling."

This saddened me. But it also explained Ava's distress at having seen her mom kissing Santa when most children would find it amusing or silly. And she said she wanted to tell someone. As close as the father and daughter had seemed to be, I was pretty sure she told him. I shoved the salad away. I couldn't eat anymore. The thought that the father could have killed Ava's mother and left his daughter without parents made my heart ache and my gut clench. I'd find a way to talk to both the father and the daughter tomorrow.

To take my mind off this new revelation, I asked, "Tell me about Tilly and Janet."

Brenda was all too happy to expound on the marriages of both women and their husbands. From what I could tell, the marriages were on the rocks before Lauren had her fun with the husbands.

I felt bad when the meal finished and Mom pulled out her card to pay. Brenda had four hard drinks, which added up to as much as another dinner. I knew Mom set up this meeting for me to get information. "I'll get the tip," I said, to help a bit with the cost.

Brenda thanked us for a lovely dinner and then tottered out of the building.

"Is she okay to drive?" I asked as we stood and put our coats on.

"She walked here. I picked this place because it is the nicest restaurant close enough for her to walk. She likes to drink in the evenings." Mom walked to the door.

I followed, wondering now how much of what Brenda said was true and how much was made up by the alcohol.

On the drive home, Mom asked, "Did you get what you needed to know?"

"Yes, and no. I hate to think Mr. Sheffield or Ava had anything to do with Lauren's death."

Mom shook her head. "Nick is too gentle a man to have killed his wife. He would have thought about the consequences if he were caught. He's not a man to do anything on the spur of the moment."

That made me feel better. But I still needed to talk to the father and daughter. "What she said about Viola. I can see her getting pissed off enough to kill Lauren if it messed up her tidy life."

Mom nodded. "Unfortunately, I can too. And I did think your sister poured it on a bit about how wonderful Kyle and Viola's marriage is. I've seen them together at events. Kyle looked as if he'd rather be somewhere else than being towed around by Viola."

I shifted in my seat to study Mom. "Do you think of the two, Viola would be the one to kill to keep her marriage safe, over Kyle killing to keep his marriage together?"

"From what I've seen, yes."

That put Viola at the top of my list. But there was Sheila, who found the body. "What about Sheila? Do you think she'd kill a woman who slept with Tom?" Seeing how her husband bossed her around, I didn't think so, but I didn't know the marriage. They were older than me in school.

"That's hard to say. On the one hand, Sheila likes to complain about Tom, but I really don't know what she'd do if she didn't help him with his job. When their kids were at home, she did everything for them, and when they left, she was lost. Helping Tom has kept her busy and happy, for the most part."

"Which would give her reason not to want another woman taking him away," I said. I liked Sheila the little bit I'd visited with her. I didn't want it to be her, but then look at all the people who had committed murder and everyone was surprised.

We arrived at my house. "Thanks for dinner and the meeting with Brenda." I opened the car door and unfolded from the small interior.

"I have a knitting class tomorrow. I'll see what I can find out from those women. You know everyone will want to talk about the murder."

"Just be careful," I said, closing the door and watching her drive away.

Lulu, Athena, and Cocoa met me at the door. I let them do their business, watching them trot around looking for the perfect spot, as the conversation at dinner played in my head.

Chapter Nine

Monday morning, I fed and checked on the outside animals and loaded up the dogs. It was rare that I didn't take the dogs with me. They were well-behaved due to their training, and they were an icebreaker if someone was having a bad day.

My first stop was the Sheffield farm. I'd looked up the address and found it was at the base of the Elkhorns out along Willow Creek. Driving up the gravel road, I was surprised that Lauren would live this far from town. She would have had a good twenty-minute to half-hour drive into town every day for work.

I parked in front of the pole fence that ran along the front of a frozen lawn and an old farmhouse. A border collie ran out from behind the house, barking. I studied my dogs in the rearview mirror. Cocoa's ears perked up as she stared at the dog. Lulu whined and wagged her tail. Athena yawned.

Opening the door, I kept an eye on the dog. He walked over to my tire and peed on it before coming over and sniffing my hand. Once introductions were finished, I walked up to the porch and front door of the house and knocked.

I could hear the faint sound of cartoons coming from inside. A quick check of my watch said if Ava was still home, she was missing school.

The door opened, and Ava stood on the other side of the screen door.

"Hi, Ava. I wondered if I could talk with you and your dad." I smiled and hoped she believed I was a friend.

"He's out feeding." She didn't offer to open the door.

"How do I find him?" I asked.

"He's in the big barn out behind the house." She glanced down at her dog, sniffing my legs. "Did you bring Athena?"

"She, Cocoa, and Lulu are all in the van." I turned sideways and waved my hand.

"Could I see Athena?" Ava asked wistfully.

"Does your dog like other dogs?" I wasn't going to take Athena out and have the border collie lay into her.

"Butch loves other dogs. But Purdy is out with Daddy, and she doesn't like other female dogs." Ava's eyes glistened with tears.

"Then I guess you'll have to sit in the van with Athena and the others while I talk to your dad."

"Really? I can go in the van?"

"As long as you remain in the seat between Athena and Lulu."

"I can do that. Let me get my boots on." Ava was in pajamas with colorful horses all over them. She ran to the back of the house and returned wearing her pink boots and a coat.

I led her out to the van and opened the sliding door. "Everyone, Ava is visiting with you for a bit. You all need to be good," I said, giving Lulu the stern eye. She liked to get carried away and lick everyone.

I helped Ava settle into the seat between the biggest and littlest dog and then pointed to the roof of what looked like a barn. "Is that where I'm headed?"

"Yep. That's the lambing barn." Ava had her arm around Athena's shoulders.

"I won't be long." I closed the door to keep the cool morning air out and walked along the dirt road beside the house toward the large barn.

Butch must have decided I needed to be tended. He trotted alongside me until an Australian Shepard charged out of the barn. She growled but didn't show her teeth.

"It's okay Purdy, I'm a friend," I said, stopping and crouching with my hand out.

"Purdy, be good!" shouted Nick as he appeared from the barn. "She won't bite, but she does make people stay their distance."

I didn't say anything about how many dogs that 'didn't bite' bit people and slowly rose to my feet after the dog had sniffed my hand and trotted back to Nick. "I hope I'm not intruding. I just wanted to see how you and Ava are doing." I did want to know that and a lot of other stuff.

When he stood in front of me, I could see he hadn't been getting enough sleep. His eyes were baggy and bloodshot. It looked as if he hadn't had the energy to shave today.

"I'll be honest, we are both still in shock." He

motioned to the house. "I was just headed in for a cup of coffee and to check on Ava."

I fell into step beside him. "Ava is in my van talking to Athena. I hope that's okay?"

"I'm glad you brought your dog with you. She has been saying she'd like to talk to Athena. I thought it was a friend and told her to give her a call. She said she couldn't because Athena couldn't hold a phone, because she didn't have hands. I was puzzled until, after more questions, I realized it was one of your dogs."

We arrived at the back of the house. "Want me to go get Ava?"

"I'm sure she'll come in when she's ready." Nick held the door open, and I walked into an updated farmhouse kitchen. If there hadn't been dishes in the sink and bowls with milk and spoons on the table, it could have been a display in a magazine.

Nick grabbed the bowls and added them to the sink. "I asked Ava to put the dishes in the dishwasher today. I hope she remembers. It's not a hard chore, but one that will help me, if she remembers."

"I'm sure there will be a lot of adjustments to make," I said, taking the seat at the table he motioned to.

"Yeah. The only good thing is I always made the coffee. Lauren couldn't function in the morning without a large cup with a fancy creamer." He placed a cup of coffee in front of me. "Do you need cream or sugar?"

"Nope. I lived in Europe for several years. Their coffee could remove paint. Then I used creamer and sugar. Here it's pretty tame. I can handle it straight." I smiled.

He studied me and sat across the table with a cup.

The cup between his hands had coffee stains on the inside and some brown dribble lines down the side. It made me cringe to think how many times that must have been drunk out of without washing it.

"Why are you interested in how Ava is doing?"

I sipped the coffee and put my cup down. "The day of the festival, she sought out Athena. While I don't think I was supposed to hear what she was saying, I did."

Nick ran a hand across the back of his neck and stared into his stained cup. "She told the dog about seeing her mom kissing Santa, didn't she?"

"Yeah, which at the time, I felt for her. I could tell she was broken up about it. After your wife's death, I heard the gossip and figured out why she was so torn up."

He nodded but didn't say anything.

"She said she was going to tell someone. Did she tell you what she saw?" I picked my cup back up and sipped, waiting.

He sighed, picked up his cup, and peered into my eyes. "Yes, she told me. I tried to make a joke of it even as my heart was cracking into pieces. I'd told Lauren if she couldn't be faithful, at least don't let Ava see her with other men."

Surprise must have shown on my face because it was something to hear a man confess to such a thing.

"Yes, I knew about all her men. When we met, she said she wanted to settle down, have a family, and live a simple life. That lasted until Ava was five. Then it was like a switch clicked in Lauren. She couldn't get enough men or sex. She tried counseling, but in a small community like this, she had to drive to Ontario to keep it secret. That's a long way to go for weekly meetings. I think she started meeting men over there instead of going to counseling." He sipped his coffee, set the cup down, and tapped his finger on the table. "I asked her if she wanted a divorce because I was getting tired of people snickering behind my back and women telling me to keep my wife away from their husbands. But she said she wanted Ava to grow up with two parents. That when she was eighteen, we'd get a divorce."

"That's ten years from now," I said, thinking how selfish in a way that was of Lauren. It might have been good for Ava to have her mother around, but not if, as she grew older, the kids started talking more and more.

He nodded. "I said don't you see what it's already doing to Ava? Lauren laughed and said she didn't have a clue. Children are more intuitive than she thought. You would think being a teacher she would have understood."

"What did you do when Ava told you about seeing Lauren with Santa?" I asked to get answers before the girl came into the house.

"I was upset that she was so foolish. I called her on her phone. She laughed and said Ava should be proud that her mom kissed Santa." He shook his head and rubbed his neck again. "She didn't get how much Ava did know. I told her I was calling an attorney and filing for divorce. That this was the last Christmas she'd get to spend in this house with her daughter. She laughed and hung up on me."

"What did you do then?" I asked.

His lips were trembling. He wiped at his eyes. "I called my friend, who is an attorney in La Grande, and asked him to start the proceedings. I'd talked to him about six months ago, and Lauren seemed to shape up, but after what Ava saw, there was no way she was going to talk me out of it this time."

"Why did you go to the Christmas tree lighting?"

He swiped at his eyes, tipped his head back, swallowed the last of his coffee, and stared into the cup. "Because it was a family tradition. After what Ava had seen, I wanted to make things normal. When Lauren didn't join us after I texted her that we were there, I figured she was mad that I had told her my lawyer was drawing up the divorce papers and would stay with one of her men. That's why when the tree didn't light, it was just one more sad thing for Ava that day. I brought her home, made her favorite caramel hot chocolate, and read her a story until she fell asleep."

"Then what did you do?"

"I tried to get some sleep. But every sound I heard, I thought it was Lauren coming home. Sheriff Skala knocked on our door at two. I had barely slept and his news…" He stared over my shoulder. "It was almost a relief. But then Ava walked in, and I had to tell her. It broke her heart. Even though Lauren couldn't stay faithful to me, she did spend time with Ava."

"You mentioned wives telling you to keep Lauren away from their husbands. Do you know their names, and were any of them recent?" I needed more names to work with. Even though my money was on Viola, sadly.

Nick tapped his finger on the table, his eyes watching the movement.

"Here you are!" Ava said, running through the back door and hugging her dad.

"I brought Ms., I'm sorry, I don't know what your last name is," Nick said.

"I'm Andi Clark. You can just call me Andi, everyone does." I smiled at Ava. "Did you and Athena have a good chat?"

Ava smiled and nodded her head. "She is so good at listening, and when she agreed with me, she winked her eye."

I smiled and grinned inside, knowing that was just one of Athena's traits. She was curious and preferred to only close one eye at a time as if she might miss something. But many people thought she was talking to them with her winks. "I'm glad she could help you with your thoughts and questions. I wanted to tell you and your dad how sorry I am for the loss of your mom." I watched the child. Her eyes glistened with unshed tears and her mouth twitched. She would miss her mom even if the woman had caused her emotional turmoil.

The tears escaped her eyes and trickled down her cheeks. She wiped at them with the back of her hands and said, "Athena agreed with me that the bad Santa must have hurt her."

I could understand the child wanting to make someone she didn't know the bad person. After all, Santa was hidden by a big red suit, cap, and long beard. He could have been anyone. I knew who the man was and intended to visit with him today.

"Did you tell that to the sheriff when he was here?" I asked.

Ava glanced at her dad, and he became interested in his empty cup.

"You didn't mention what you saw that day to the sheriff? How is he to know to look for that person if you didn't say anything?" I couldn't believe the two had kept that information from the police. "You need to call him and give a statement about what Ava saw. It's evidence."

"Are you a policeman?" Ava asked, her eyes wide.

"No, I'm not. But I've been involved in several investigations through my past work, and I know when something is evidence and what you saw is." I glanced at Nick. He was nodding but not meeting my gaze.

"Why wouldn't you tell the police everything you know?" I didn't understand his holding back. Unless he knew who Santa was and planned his own revenge.

"What's the point of dragging Ava into this? He'll dig up enough of my wife's fooling around to come to the same conclusion." Nick raised his gaze and added. "She's been through enough because of Lauren. She doesn't need to be the main witness in her mother's death."

Chapter Ten

I drove away from the Sheffield farm, wondering at
the man's determination to shield his daughter when she
already knew everything. I glanced at Athena in the
rearview mirror. "Did you and Ava have a good chat?"
Athena winked. I chuckled and hoped Nick followed
through with sending me the names of the wives who
had harassed him about keeping Lauren away from
their men.

The plan was to drive straight to the real estate
office where Kyle and Viola worked. But since Nick
had withheld information when Sheriff Skala
interviewed him, and I knew that, I didn't want the
sheriff to find out I knew something and was holding
back. Reluctantly, I decided to try to catch the sheriff.

I parked near the low brown building to the side of
the courthouse. My phone rang as I turned to talk to the
dogs. "Hello?"

"It's Betty. I overheard something this morning that
might be of interest to your investigation." The lilt in

her voice made me smile.

"What did you hear?"

"A couple of men in the bakery this morning wondered where their wives were when Lauren was killed."

"Oh, wow! Do you know who the men were?" If I had the names, I could give them to Bailey, and she could give those and the information I got from Mr. Sheffield to the sheriff.

"I asked Janie who was sitting at the table near me. They were Rod Evers and Lyle Mason."

"That's good work. I'll pass the names on to my niece, Bailey. I'm trying to stay out of the sheriff's radar."

"Why is that?" Betty asked.

"He made it plain that I'm not to be nosing around in his homicide. It could put me or the people I talk to in danger." I scoffed at the end. I knew how to conduct an investigation.

"He could be right," Betty said.

"Wait a minute. Are you going to help me? If not, I'll keep my thoughts and information to myself." I wanted to have someone to bounce things off of. It was how Mick and I worked, but I didn't want that person telling me all the time that what I was doing could be dangerous. It was only dangerous when you were sloppy. I didn't plan to be sloppy.

"I'm going to help you if for no other reason than to make sure you are safe. But I also want to help Ava and Nick. They are good people who were living with a witch of a mother and wife."

Betty didn't normally say anything bad about people. Hearing her talk this way about the deceased told me a lot about Lauren Sheffield.

"Thank you. I'm getting ready to take the dogs for a walk and see if I can find Bailey, then I'm going to have a chat with Kyle Stevens."

"I'll meet you at the real estate office. I'd like to get a look at his aura," Betty said with a lot more enthusiasm than she'd had earlier.

"You still haven't told me how you 'see' the aura," I said, again wondering about how a blind woman could see color.

"It's hard to explain. I took a fall about five years ago. After that, I noticed when people talked and I faced them, I'd see an egg-shaped color where I imagine they were standing." Betty sighed. "I asked an eye doctor about it. He said it was just my ocular nerve had been jiggled and it would go away." Betty started with a new vigor. "But it didn't go away. The colors became stronger the longer I faced the person. So, I started asking the computer about seeing egg-shaped colors, and that's when I learned about auras, and realized the colors I see are people's auras. Then I talked to a person who specializes in reading auras. She would look at a person and then face me toward them. I'd tell her what I saw, and she confirmed that's what I can do, even though I can't see the person. It's their energy that is somehow making it into my senses by facing them, and I see their auras."

I was stunned at what a fall had done to my friend. "That is the most unusual thing I've ever heard. And believe me, traveling around the world like Mick and I did, we saw a lot of things that couldn't be explained. I'm happy that you have this ability."

"It has been a help in some way and a bit of a

hindrance in others. I have to go. I'll meet you at the real estate office." Betty ended the call, leaving me staring at my cell phone.

I shook my head, smiled, and peered over my shoulder at the dogs. "Let's see if we can find Bailey." Their eyes brightened, and Lulu gave a short bark. I hooked their leashes onto them, and we walked up to the building that housed the sheriff's office.

All my years growing up, I'd not been in the building. It looked as old on the inside as it did on the outside. It was fitting, I guess, that the building looked as old as the stone courthouse next door, which dated to 1862 when the first gold was found in the area and Auburn was a booming gold town.

"Can I help you?" asked a woman about my age from behind a window.

"I'd like to speak to Deputy Harper," I said.

"She's not in. I can have her call you." She poised a pen over a pink 'While you were out' pad.

"Can you tell me where she is?" I didn't want to wait to tell her what I'd learned. "Or I can give her a call, I have her phone number."

The woman studied me. "Who are you?"

"Andi Clark. I'm Deputy Harper's aunt."

The woman closed the metal portal that allowed our voices to carry back and forth and picked up the phone. She spoke into it, nodded, then replaced the receiver and opened the portal. "She said she'll meet you at the park."

I smiled and said, "Thank you."

Standing on the sidewalk, I said, "Looks like you will get a walk and I'll get to visit with Bailey."

Cocoa gave a small woof, Athena winked, and

Lulu did her happy sneeze. I laughed and walked to the park.

When we reached the edge of the park, I spotted Bailey walking across the dying grass toward us. After my group stopped and peed, she met us not thirty feet from the street.

Bailey nodded toward Bow Wow Brew. "Want to talk over coffee?"

"Sure." We walked to the road, waited for cars to pass, and crossed. I went to our usual table in the corner of the patio and told the dogs to stay.

Bailey patted them each on their head and followed me to the window to order. "I wish my dog obeyed as well as yours do," she said, following me.

"You have to be around your dog as many hours a day as I am to train him. Do you want a coffee?" I asked, walking up to the window.

Stacy, the mid-day window person, smiled. "Do you want your usual?"

"Yes, please. And Bailey will have a coffee."

"And a turkey sandwich, please," Bailey said, smiling, her hands in her coat pockets.

"Add the turkey sandwich." I paid, Stacy handed me three pup cups, and we went back to the table to wait for the order.

When we were seated, I held a pup cup up for everyone to get a lick.

"Why did you need to see me?" Bailey asked and sipped her coffee.

I glanced around to make sure no one was close enough to hear. "I checked on Ava this morning and discovered that they didn't tell the sheriff about her seeing her mom kissing Santa and her telling her dad."

Bailey leaned forward. "That is interesting." Her eyes narrowed. "Why did you go there, and why are you telling me?"

I ignored her accusing tone and gave the crunchy cone to Athena before holding up another pup cup for each dog to lick. "Because I wanted to make sure Ava was doing okay. And your boss told me not to be snooping around in his investigation." I stopped when Stacy brought over the sandwiches.

"Thank you," Bailey said and handed her five dollars. When the waitress left, she studied me. "Why are you snooping around in his investigation?"

"Because I don't think Nick killed his wife, and I don't think your new boss will look any further than the spouse."

Bailey smiled. "Most homicides are committed by the spouse."

I shook my head. "Not in this homicide. After Nick confronted his wife about allowing their daughter to see her kissing someone else, he called his lawyer and told him to move forward on filing for divorce. Does that sound like a man who killed his wife?"

"He could have told you that to get you feeling sorry for him." Bailey unwrapped her sandwich.

I slid the business card Nick gave me across the table. "Call the lawyer and ask."

She glanced down at the card, then picked it up, slipping it into her jacket pocket. "How am I going to tell Sheriff Skala that I've been digging into the homicide when he sent me out to check on a cut fence?"

"Tell him you happened to be going by the Sheffield place and dropped by to see how they were doing. Nick started talking, and you listened." I shrugged and bit into my sandwich.

"But what if he's just playing you? That would mean he's feeding you only evidence that will make him look innocent." Bailey put the sandwich down and peered into my eyes.

"I believe he's innocent, but you need to either get the truth out of him about what happened or talk your boss into going to talk to him again. He didn't tell Sheriff Skala what he told me because he didn't want Ava drawn into the investigation."

Bailey picked her sandwich back up and asked, "Why do you care that the man is innocent?"

"Ava lost her mother. I want to make sure she doesn't lose her father if he didn't do it. It's the girl I care about." My past was dictating my decisions about this. I knew that and wasn't about to confess that to my niece.

"Compassion is a good thing to have, but you have to put it to the side when it comes to finding a murderer." Bailey wiped her mouth, rolled up the paper her sandwich had been wrapped in, and stood. "I've learned you can't afford to have sympathy for anyone connected to the crime. As law enforcement, I have to be impartial and find the truth."

I nodded and added, "You might press Nick for the names of the women who told him to keep his wife away from their husbands. I asked for the list, but the conversation changed when Ava entered the room." I broke the dog cookie into large, medium, and small pieces and fed it to the dogs.

"You know I should be telling you to stop investigating, but I have a feeling the accountant in you who likes to have everything add up will just keep digging." Bailey finished off her coffee. "If you are going to continue to dig, bring everything to me. I'll find a way to get it to the sheriff."

I smiled. "Thank you. I'm not new to being careful when I'm investigating someone. It's kind of what Mick and I did for twenty years."

"That was with numbers. This is people. Whenever you deal with people, you don't know what the outcome will be." Bailey stepped toward me with her arms outstretched.

I walked into her hug. "I know all about people. I promise to bring everything to you."

Bailey stepped back. "Thank you for the information. I'll let you know if the sheriff does anything with it."

"Thanks."

She turned and walked out the patio entrance.

I patted Cocoa's head. "Let's finish your walk, and then meet up with Betty to visit Kyle."

❀ ❀ ❀

After a walk around the park and chasing squirrels, I loaded the dogs back up and drove to the Stevens and Waller Real Estate office. Parking, I could see through the plate-glass window that Viola was there. Betty was also already inside, sitting on a cushioned bench inside the door. Swallowing the lump in my throat, I entered and smiled.

"Andi, don't tell me you want to move away from your family again?" Viola said, with her usual taunting tone.

I kept the smile on my face, releasing my clenched teeth. "I'm not moving anywhere. I'm back for good."

Betty popped up from the bench. "Good, you made it."

I walked over and took Betty by the elbow.

"Just follow my lead," she whispered. In a louder voice, she said, "See, I told you Andi was coming to meet me to help me look for a new house. Kyle was supposed to put together some suggestions for me."

I led her over toward Viola. I was glad that Betty couldn't see the distaste on the woman's face.

I glanced around and didn't see anyone else. "Any chance we could catch up to Kyle somewhere?"

Viola's shark smile disappeared and her eyes narrowed. "If Kyle put something together for Betty, he would have told me. What are you really doing here? Nina said you were sticking your nose into Lauren's death."

A smile of satisfaction was hard to hide. She'd just linked her husband to Lauren's death. "I'm here to help Betty. But I was curious as to why Lauren asked him to be Santa and why he did it."

Viola tipped her head, studying me. "Why would you want to know that?"

"To see if she mentioned why she took that job away from her boss." By spinning it toward Waldo Dennis, I hoped to lower her guard and Kyle's.

"Oh! I see. You think Waldo killed her." Viola sat on the corner of a desk with her nameplate on it. "I do know that he's been trying to get her interested in him. Did you know that he nominated her for Teacher of the Year?" Viola snorted. "She was the worst teacher at the high school."

"How do you know that?" Maybe if I kept her talking, Kyle would arrive.

"Her first year was our Dylan's Freshman year. From what he, his friends, and parents I've talked to said, you can bet there is no way she'd have even been in the running. All she did was assign the class to read the book, then she handed out tests. She never taught or gave lectures. Just sat at her desk reading or on her phone, while the class read the book." Viola stood and pointed at me. "And not a single student in her class failed. They all received Cs and above. I don't think she even scored the tests. I think she just gave the students she liked an A, mostly the boys, the smart girls Bs, and the rest Cs."

I didn't know Lauren but from what I'd been learning, that seemed about right. "Have you heard any gossip about Waldo and Lauren?"

Viola sat back on the desk and studied her pristinely manicured nails. "Nothing other than her nomination."

"Thanks. Where can I find Kyle? You know, to ask him if he found any possibilities for Betty."

"He's showing a house on Settler Street. One-thirty-four."

"Thank you."

My hand was on the door when she called out, "Hey, why are you so interested in Lauren's death?"

I spun around and said, "I want to make sure Ava gets closure and doesn't hear her mom's name dragged through the mud."

Viola's face paled. No doubt she had been spreading nasty rumors around about the dead woman. Not thinking about the child left behind. That was Viola, never thinking about others, only her own personal joy at bringing everyone else down.

Chapter Eleven

Betty insisted on joining me in tracking down Kyle. I loaded her into the passenger seat and headed for Settler Street. I spotted the SUV with the real estate agency name painted on the side two blocks down from Main Street. I parked behind it and waited for Kyle to finish up his business with the potential buyers. When he approached his vehicle, I stepped out of the van, with Betty in my wake, and called to him.

Kyle faced me. His gaze went from me to Betty and back to me. He smiled. "The lady with the petting zoo," he said, walking toward me.

I held out my hand to shake. "Andi Clark, I'm Nina Harper's sister."

His posture tightened and he peered over my shoulder at Betty. "I've heard a lot about you. I didn't know you and Blind Betty were friends."

I scowled at his derogatory remark about Betty. When we were in school, the kids had called her that until I punched a boy in the nose. "She is my friend, and you'll call her Betty. What you heard about me might or might not be true, depending on who you were talking to," I said.

"My wife doesn't like you very much." He leaned his butt against my van and folded his arms, studying me. He was trying to look nonchalant, but I could see the muscle in his cheek twitching.

"It's mutual. I'm not a fan of hers either. I wanted to know if Lauren told you why she needed a Santa when Waldo Dennis had been Santa for the last couple of years?" Might as well dive right into my questions since he had Viola's prejudice to sort through.

"We, Lauren and I, were at a meeting. I made the crack, I wondered what it would be like to dress up as Santa and have all those kids excited to see me. Our kids are grown, and so far, no grandkids. I miss having the little ones around." He said this, then peered at me as if he thought I'd make some smart-aleck crack.

"What was her reply?" I asked.

"She said, if she could get me the gig, would I follow through and do it? I told her yes. Next thing I know, she brings me a Santa suit and tells me when and where to show up. And it was fun until…" His eyes widened, and then the eyelids dropped, hiding any emotion that might have shone. His body grew even more rigid.

"Until what?" I asked.

"I already told Sheriff Skala about the arguments. Why are you asking me?" He shoved away from the van and walked toward his vehicle.

"Did she argue with Waldo?" I asked.

He spun around. "Yeah. He was furious that I was playing Santa. I didn't know he hadn't been told about it. Later Sheila came in and started in on me and then Lauren, saying it was a cruel thing to do to Waldo. Lauren laughed at her and said it was about time Waldo realized he didn't get everything he wanted. When I asked her what she meant by that, she just shrugged."

"So both Waldo and Sheila were upset with Lauren?"

"That's putting it lightly. They both looked as if they would have killed her if I hadn't been standing there." He realized what he said, and backtracked. "I mean, they were both pretty mad. Not that I think either one of them would have laid a hand on her."

I nodded. "I know what you meant. Thanks." Filing away what he said, I grasped Betty by the elbow and led her back to the van.

"I know Viola has had it in for you forever. Do you know why?" Betty asked.

"I don't have a clue. But I'm pretty sure Viola is who made Nina not like me. I remember a time when we played together and had fun. Then, all of a sudden, she started shunning me. I don't know why." I had thought about this a lot over the years, yearning for a sister whom I could confide in and laugh with. But Nina kept me at a distance. It hurt. To change the subject, I said, "What did you think of Kyle's answer?"

"He was holding something back. His aura was giving off mixed messages. He was curious about you, but also wary."

"I got all of that, too. Which isn't surprising

considering who he is married to. I'm headed to the shop now. Where can I drop you off?" I needed to stop in and work on the books. After today, I'd be pretty busy the rest of the week.

"I'll walk home from the shop. It's not far, and I'm used to walking around Auburn. I've been doing it my whole life."

I heard the bit of melancholy in her voice. "Did you enjoy traveling when you went to Ethiopia?"

"I did. I can see why you didn't come home and traveled with Mick. If I had a companion to travel with, I would be basking in sunshine during the winter months."

"That sounds like fun. We'll have to see if we can find you one."

Betty laughed, and I parked in the lot behind the old building on Main Street, where my family sold spun wool and items made from the wool.

"I'll give you a call if I learn anything else," Betty said, walking away from the lot using her colorful cane.

"Sounds good," I replied, unharnessing the dogs and hooking a leash to their collars.

Once we entered the back door, I unleashed the dogs. They all trotted over to their beds in the back of the large open area where my bookkeeping desk stood. In the far corner, Nina sat at the spinning wheel, making yarn. Mom was in her cozy chair surrounded by six folding chairs and her knitting students. The sound of the weaving loom clunking upstairs told me that Rudy was weaving.

I walked to the cash register, pulled out the receipts from the week before, and went back to my desk. I spent the next hour adding up the receipts and checking the amounts with the bank deposit on Friday. Stretching, I stood and watched Mom's students roll up their yarn, tucking it and the knitting needles in their bags.

She'd tried to teach me to knit years ago but I didn't have the patience or the interest.

"Turn the pot on," she said to me as she followed her students to the door, encouraging them to keep knitting between the meetings.

I walked over to the counter, where we had a sink, a small refrigerator, and a hot pot to warm up water for tea, hot chocolate, or instant coffee. I filled the pot and flicked the switch. Glancing over my shoulder, I asked Nina, "Do you want anything?"

She ignored me. I wondered if Viola had called and complained about my visit.

I went to the bottom of the stairs and called up to Rudy. "Do you want to take a break and have tea?"

The rhythmic sound stopped and footsteps thumped above my head.

I returned to the counter and plopped tea bags in three cups. When the switch clicked off, I poured the water. By then, Mom had three napkins on the table and placed a cupcake on each one. I glanced over at the dog beds and found three sets of eyes watching the table.

Rudy emerged from the stairway and plopped on the closest chair. I waited for Mom to sit, knowing she would sit in front of the cupcake she wanted. When she was seated, I walked over with my cup of tea and sat. The cupcake in front of me was my favorite, carrot cake. I glanced at Rudy's half-eaten cupcake and saw it was his favorite. Mom was peeling the wrapper off her favorite. She had it all planned. I wondered if Nina's favorite cupcake was still in the box.

"What did you learn today?" Mom asked.

I flicked a glance at Nina and said, "I visited with Nick and Ava this morning and discovered they didn't tell Sheriff Skala everything. I suggested he go in and do that. Then I met with Bailey and told her what I'd learned." I sipped my hot tea and broke my cupcake in two before continuing. "At the real estate office, I talked with Viola."

"You mean harassed her," Nina spoke up from the spinning wheel.

"No, I asked her how Lauren had talked Kyle into being Santa. After talking to Kyle, it turns out Lauren gave him the job of Santa to make Waldo mad. The more I find out about Lauren, the more I dislike her." If I had known her, she would have been one of the people I managed to avoid. I have never liked negative people in my life. That was why I had always given my sister space. She was too negative for my liking.

"Do you still think Kyle or Viola killed Lauren?" Nina asked.

When I didn't answer quickly with a 'no,' Nina stood up with her hands on her hips. "I can't work in the same building as you. I'm going home. One of you will have to give Mom a ride home." She grabbed her coat and purse and stomped out the back door of the building.

I glanced at Mom. Her eyes held sadness.

She shook her head at me and smiled. "She'll be okay. Why she has always thought the sun rises and sets with Viola, I'll never know. The woman is toxic."

I agreed and bit into my cupcake.

"Does this mean I can have Nina's cupcake?" Rudy

asked.

Mom waved a hand toward the box, and he jumped out of his chair, crossing the space in two strides.

I laughed, and the tension eased. "I didn't want to say it in front of Nina, but Kyle was really tense while we talked. He slipped out something that I think was supposed to throw me off of him."

Rudy leaned forward. "What was it?"

I told him about Kyle saying Waldo and Sheila had come in and argued with Lauren. "He made it sound like a slip. Like he didn't think either of them were capable of killing her. But the look in his eyes. It was almost as if he wanted me to believe one of them did it."

"Like he was sending you on a witch hunt," Mom said, shaking her head.

"Yeah. But he also started to say something that made me think he wasn't happy with Lauren either. But he stopped himself before saying it exactly. I believe Nick told Lauren about filing for a divorce when she was with Kyle." I picked up the second half of my cupcake and studied it. "I wonder if she said something like 'if you get a divorce, we could get married.'" I glanced at Mom and then Rudy. "That would mean Kyle could lose his interest in the real estate agency, his wife, his house, and who knows what his kids would think of him."

"I see where you're going with this," Rudy said, having finished off Nina's treat. "I could ask Carson Drexler. He's friends with Kyle. Maybe he knows if Kyle was hot and heavy with Lauren or just a brief fling, and if Kyle made some comment about Lauren asking him to get a divorce."

"You can't just ask him those things," I said, seeing Rudy coming home with a black eye or ending up in jail from a bar brawl. "If they are best friends, this Carson will figure out what you're trying to do."

"Monica is friends with Carson's wife. We'll go out for dinner or something like that, and I'll just drop a few wrong comments and see if Carson or his wife replies." He shrugged.

"I don't know…" I picked at my cupcake, wanting to tell him to go ahead, but not wanting Mom to think I was sending her baby into trouble.

"That's a good idea," Mom said, patting Rudy's arm. Her enthusiastic acceptance of Rudy's plan surprised me.

"Are you sure, Mom?" I asked.

"Yes. The sooner we can find the answers, the sooner everyone in Auburn will feel safe again. Nearly everyone in my knitting circle mentioned how the death of Lauren has made them scared to be out at night and worried about attending the rescheduled tree lighting. We have to get this cleared up so people can enjoy the holidays." She bit into her cupcake and chewed, her gaze flitting back and forth between me and Rudy.

"What about Nina? You know she isn't going to like us continuing to dig into Viola and Kyle's lives." I wasn't worried about her anger toward me. I only come into the shop a few times a week, but Mom and Rudy had to deal with her every day.

"If one of them is a murderer, Nina will have to reconcile herself to the fact that she has been idolizing the wrong people." Mom finished her cupcake and brushed her hands together. "I'm going to wash up and finish that hat I'm making. Rudy can take me home.

You go ahead and do more sleuthing, or go home yourself and take care of your animals. Don't you have to be somewhere with them tomorrow?"

I stared at Mom. Did I? Then I remembered the Christian church had asked if I could bring Sparky around for an audition to be the donkey for their nativity scene the week of Christmas. "Thanks, Mom! I almost forgot about that." I hugged her and thanked Rudy for helping to uncover information. Then I gathered up my dogs and we walked down the street to the dog park. I let them run free and do their business while I ran all the information I'd gathered around in my head.

Chapter Twelve

I wanted to ask Sheila about her argument with Lauren the day she died. "Are you all ready?" I called. Athena plodded over to me, Cocoa ran from the far side back to me, and Lulu made circles and sniffed along the fence, eventually arriving at my feet. "You took your time," I said, picking her up and hugging her. "If you weren't so cute, I'd trade you in for a bigger model."

She licked the side of my face and looked at me with her big, brown and gold eyes. I knew no matter how much she did her own thing, I'd still keep her. I put their leashes on and we headed back to the wool shop and the van. After they were loaded, I drove over to the City Hall and parked close to the front entrance.

"I'll be right back, and we'll go home. I want to talk to someone." I exited my vehicle and walked up the steps of the newly built City Hall. When I was a kid, the city shared a building with the city police. Since the city police force downsized, they moved into the Sheriff's office. The old City Hall was bulldozed and the new one was built on the same lot.

I waved at Margo, a woman I went to school with, and continued down the hall to the mayor's office. When I first arrived back in Auburn, I visited with Mayor Graham to see how I could benefit the city with my therapy animals. Then I went to the county commissioner and visited with him. I wanted to make sure that when I approached schools and nursing homes, they knew I was a legitimate therapy animal handler.

"Andi, I don't have you down for a meeting with Tom," Sheila said as I entered the office.

"I don't have an appointment. I wondered if I could take you to have coffee?" I smiled and tried not to appear over-eager, even though I really didn't want to talk to her in this office with her husband behind the door.

She studied me, then glanced at the appointment book on her desk. "I could take my break early. The sandwich shop down the street is close enough that I can get back in time for his next meeting."

"Sounds good." I waited for her to let Tom know she was going out for coffee, put on her coat, and pick up her purse. "I enjoy a walk in the afternoon. It wakes me up," she said as we stepped out into a cold, brisk wind.

"I think we're going to get our first snow of the year soon," I said, keeping up with her quick strides.

"I hope so. I love it when there's snow for

Christmas."

We arrived at the sandwich shop and went in. The time of day left us with a choice of seating. Walking up to the counter, I noticed Viola's cousin Emily making sandwiches. Once we had our drinks, I directed Sheila to a table near the front of the building to keep Emily from hearing our conversation.

"What did you want to talk to me about? I'm doing fine. The initial shock of finding Lauren like that is wearing off," Sheila started.

"That's good to hear, but I'm sure coming across something like that has to linger," I said, sipping chai tea.

"It was horrible to walk around the pavilion and find her, like that, you know." Sheila had her hands wrapped around her cup of coffee.

"What was your first thought when you saw her lying there?" I asked, and wasn't surprised when her eyes narrowed as she studied me.

"I was shocked and horrified." Sheila picked up her coffee and held it in front of her face as she sipped.

"You weren't slightly happy that she wouldn't be interfering with the Christmas Festival anymore?" I asked.

She set her coffee down so hard that some spurted out of the drinking hole on the lid. "That's ridiculous. Why would I think that?"

"Because she made herself in charge of the Santa and didn't keep you in the loop that she wasn't using Waldo." I kept my gaze on her, watching, hoping she'd do something that would tell me if she killed Lauren.

"I didn't tell her she had to keep me in the loop. When she volunteered, she gave me the impression that she'd offered to take over to help her chances for Teacher of the Year. I didn't expect her to shut out Waldo when he was the one who nominated her." Sheila cleaned up the mess she'd made from slamming her cup on the table, and said quietly, "When I saw her latest conquest walk up to the pavilion carrying that Santa suit. I couldn't believe it. First, I thought, oh, he just brought that in for Waldo to wear, but then I saw her helping him into it." Sheila's cheeks reddened. "They were practically making out behind the sleigh. It was disgusting. Their behavior wasn't what we want at a family event."

"What did you do about it?" I asked.

"I called Tom and told him what I saw. He said he'd take care of it and to not allow that woman to volunteer for anything again. I went off to check on all the booths. On my way back to the pavilion, Waldo came storming down the sidewalk. I stopped him. He was so upset, he could hardly put two words together." She swallowed coffee and continued, "He kept mumbling 'and all I've done for her.' I didn't know what he was talking about, but I could tell not being Santa had upset him. I told him I'd be taking the job back next year, and he would be Santa. He nodded and walked away. I was furious and went in to tell both of them off, not only for taking Waldo's job away from him but because of their behavior. Kyle looked upset when I walked up. He became more agitated as I talked. Lauren just smiled as if she'd gotten away with something and said, 'You can have your job and your husband back, you old cow.'"

I set my cup down and stared at her in astonishment. "Had Tom been one of her conquests?"

At this point, I was happy I didn't have a husband. It seemed no one was off limits to Lauren. Even though I knew Mick wouldn't have fallen for her. He'd dealt with many women like her in his job and always told me he was happy to come home to a genuine woman.

"I don't think so. I think she just said that to rile me up more or make me go ask him."

"Did you? Ask him?" I asked, watching all the emotions rolling across her face and sparking in her eyes.

"No. I didn't want to give the woman the benefit of thinking I didn't trust my husband." Sheila picked up her drink.

"When was the last time you saw Lauren alive?" I asked.

"Now you sound like the sheriff. What do you care?" Sheila studied me.

"I'm trying to make everyone in town feel safe enough to come to the next tree lighting. I want to find the killer." I did want to find the killer and make my community feel safe. But I also wanted to prove to myself that I could solve a murder.

"People don't want to come because of Lauren?" Sheila's eyes glistened with tears. "I should have told her no when she wanted to volunteer. I thought it was a bad idea, but Tom said to give her the benefit of the doubt and see if she could become a volunteer resource."

My radar started beeping. Tom had urged Sheila to give Lauren the job. Lauren told her that she'd been sleeping with Sheila's husband. I concentrated on Sheila's body language and asked her the same question again. "Are you sure you didn't mention to Tom what

Lauren had said about him?"

Sheila's back straightened and she glared at me. "No, I didn't say a word."

She was upset but didn't seem to be lying. "Okay. Thank you for visiting with me."

"I think Viola is the one who killed her," Sheila said in a quiet voice.

I leaned closer, realizing she knew that Emily was Viola's cousin. "What makes you say that?"

"She popped in to see how Kyle was doing as Santa. It was when I went off to call Tom about their behavior. I have a feeling she saw Kyle and Lauren making out."

This was something I needed to confirm with other people before I brought the information to the sheriff. "I'd like to go back to the office with you and get a copy of the vendors. I want to talk to the ones who were the closest to the pavilion."

"We can go now. I need to get back." Sheila stood.

I followed her out the door. Before stepping away from the building, I glanced through the large window and spotted Emily watching us.

This new information was damaging to Viola. I needed to talk to the vendors and see if anyone remembered seeing Viola near the pavilion or around the Santa photo shoot area. I couldn't have Bailey give the information to Sheriff Skala about this until I had more to back up what Sheila said. She could have just thrown me a bone to get me away from Tom and Lauren.

At City Hall, I peeked at the appointment book on Sheila's desk while she went in search of a map with all the vendors. It appeared that the mayor had a meeting at the J & P Bakery the following morning. I'd have to load up Sparky early for his audition and have him wait in the van while I talked to the mayor after his meeting.

Sheila walked back into the room with a paper in her hand. "I hope you can clear this up before Saturday. I would hate for people to not attend the tree lighting thinking it was unsafe."

"Thanks. I'll see what I can do." I took the paper from her and left the building. I figured the dogs had waited for me long enough. I unlocked the door and settled in the driver's seat before turning and checking on my passengers. They were all curled up asleep. They each opened one eye when I spoke to them. "Let's go home and check on the rest of the crew."

They sat up and made happy noises as I pulled away from the curb. I'd spend the evening figuring out which people to talk to about seeing Viola in the Santa area.

Chapter Thirteen

The following morning, Sparky was easy to load up. He was always interested in seeing new things, but he became agitated when he realized he was the only one going. Deciding Cocoa would be the best van buddy for him, I went into the house and put her harness on.

Athena started to rise. I told her to stay. "You and Lulu can hang out in the house until I bring Sparky back. I'll be back by lunch."

She plopped back down on her bed. Lulu studied me from her dog bed on the couch. I patted her head and told her she was a good girl before leaving the house with Cocoa.

Sparky's high-pitched braying could be heard clear to the house when I stepped out. "That is why you are going along. I don't need him making all this racket while I try to talk to Mayor Graham," I said to Cocoa.

I opened the sliding door on the van and Sparky

stopped braying. He watched as I loaded up Cocoa and hooked her harness to the lead on the seatbelt. "I brought you company. Now be good. You don't want to mess up your audition with the church." I closed the sliding door and went around to the driver's door.

After settling into the seat, I glanced in the rearview mirror. Sparky was sniffing Cocoa through the wire panel between them. "Don't bite her hair or you'll not have company again." I put the van in drive and we headed to town.

I arrived at the bakery as multiple people were walking out. I quickly locked the van and hurried in to catch Tom before he left. He sat at a table where it was obvious by the empty cups and saucers around the table that the other people had been sitting with him.

Slipping into the chair across from Tom, I raised a hand to catch the girl's attention behind the counter. "I'll have a hot chocolate and a chocolate éclair, please."

Tom glanced up from where he'd been writing. He smiled, but the smile didn't light up his eyes. "Andi, what are you doing out and about so early?"

"I wanted to have a chat with you. I'm on my way to take Sparky to a nativity audition at the Christian church." I thanked the girl who brought me the drink and éclair. When she was back behind the counter, I leaned forward. "I had a long chat with Sheila yesterday."

"Yes, she told me." He pulled off his glasses and wiped them with a handkerchief.

"Did she tell you about the part where Lauren said you and she were lovers?" I leaned back and sipped my hot chocolate, watching his face grow redder and redder.

His eyes bulged as he leaned across the table. "I did not have an affair with Lauren. I can't believe you would even suggest such a thing. Sheila and I are happy. I wouldn't go looking for anything else."

"Why do you think Lauren said that to Sheila?" I picked up the éclair and took a bite. It was delicious as always.

"Because she liked to make trouble. I'm surprised she lasted as long as she did at the high school. She was always poking people, getting them angry, and pitting them against one another."

"Did you know that Waldo had a thing for Lauren, and she just poured salt into his wounds over and over again?" I asked. Last night, as I went through the vendor names, I wondered why Sheila had championed Waldo so vehemently. I called Mom and found out that they were siblings.

"Yes, I know about my brother-in-law's infatuation with Lauren. I didn't see it, but I'm a happily married man. Waldo has been lonely since his wife passed. I think Waldo was blind to her evilness because he wanted her to like him."

"So much so, he nominated her for Teacher of the Year. I understand she wouldn't qualify if someone had looked into her teaching habits." I took another bite and chewed, watching him rub a hand over his face.

"True. I couldn't believe it when I saw the nomination. There were half a dozen other teachers who could win it, but he picked the least likely one. When I asked him why, he said, Lauren promised to go out to dinner with him." Tom shook his head. "I had always thought Waldo was level-headed and old-fashioned. But for some reason, Lauren shook his world and he wanted her."

"Did he say anything to you about not being asked to be Santa?" I finished off the pastry and sipped my hot chocolate.

"He came to me after he'd been to the pavilion and talked to Lauren. Sounded like she pretty much just shoved his face in it. He was furious and disappointed. She finally came off the pedestal he'd placed her on."

I sat up straighter. "He was disillusioned?"

"So much so that when Sheila told me who was killed, I called to tell him, and he said it was for the best." Tom had been tapping a pen on the notebook in front of him. He stopped and peered at me. "That doesn't mean he did it. Even with all the mean things she did to him, Waldo doesn't have it in him to take a life. I tried to take him hunting once. He couldn't pull the trigger when he had the buck in his sights."

"But the buck hadn't made a fool of him," I said. "Thank you for your time and the conversation. I have to get Sparky to his audition." As if he heard his name, a high-pitched bray rattled the bakery windows.

I hurried out the door and found some middle school kids knocking on the windows and making faces at Sparky. "Hey, get away and leave him alone, or I'll let him out to get you for taunting him."

The kids took off, and Sparky settled down. I glanced at Cocoa's seat and found her with her paws over her head.

I unlocked the van and twisted to pet Cocoa. "Sorry about that. I'll give you earplugs next time." She licked my hand and sat up. I made eye contact with Sparky. "You better be on your best behavior when we get to the church. Otherwise, you'll miss out on hanging out with other people for several days."

The Christian Church was on the west side of town, at the edge of a large field. Several horse trailers with cows, donkeys, and sheep tied to them were parked near the back of the church. I decided that must be where they were going to pick the animals.

Parking, I spotted Trish Marlow, the woman who had called and asked me to bring Sparky. She walked over to the van as I exited and said, "If you can bring your donkey over by the nativity scene, we want to see how he'll behave with the wooden structures, the cow we've chosen, and the sheep."

"I'll get him." I went to the back of the van, opened the doors, lowered the ramp, and swung the gate open. Sparky walked up to me, and I put the lead rope on him. He walked down the ramp as if he were the king of all the donkeys. When he stood on the ground, he raised his nose, curled his upper lip, and showed off his yellow teeth.

I chuckled and led him over to the nativity scene. He walked alongside me with his ears forward, curious about everything. That was one of Sparky's best traits; he was curious and therefore never balked at anything different. This made him a good prospect for a therapy animal.

"If you could lead him by the cow, the sheep, and the manger, please," Trish said as everyone watched.

I walked slowly, leading Sparky. He glanced at the cow and the sheep, but he stopped mand looked into the manger, most likely hoping for a snack. I only had to give a little tug on the rope, and he started walking.

"Nice, he does seem to be docile." Trish turned to a

man in insulated coveralls. "Mark, you take the rope and lead him past everything and see how he does with someone he doesn't know."

I handed the rope to Mark and stood by Trish.

"Mark will be playing Joseph. He will be leading your donkey."

"He's too small for Mary to be riding on him," I said.

"She won't be. It's just a symbolism of the donkey that brought her to the stable."

Mark had led Sparky out around everyone standing there and then walked by the cow, the sheep, and at the manger, Sparky again stopped and looked in before walking past.

"Isn't that cute how he looks in the manger every time!" one of the women exclaimed. "I say he's the one."

Everyone started talking at once. I kept an eye on Sparky and wasn't shocked when I noticed a blue bandanna hanging from his mouth. It had been in the back pocket of Mark's overalls. I walked over and grabbed the bandanna. "Let go," I said in a whisper in Sparky's ear.

He shook his head, trying to pull the cloth from my hand.

"Let it go, or you won't get any grain tonight." I glared into his eyes, and he unclenched his teeth, letting the bandanna dangle in my hand.

"Hey! How'd you get my bandanna?" Mark asked.

I patted Sparky's head. "Word of warning, if you pick him. He is a thief. If there is something that isn't attached, he will take it."

And of course, Sparky stood there looking at

everyone with big, brown, innocent eyes.

"I don't believe such a handsome fella as this would be a thief. And his stopping at the manger will make everyone's heart melt." Trish stroked one of Sparky's long ears. "We have to try out the other two donkeys. You can stay and watch, or I'll call you with the results later."

"If you're going to do the other donkeys now, we'll wait and watch." Sparky raised his nose and showed his teeth. I took that to mean he wanted to see his competition.

The other two donkeys appeared calm. However, one balked and wouldn't walk to the sheep, no matter how much the owner talked and made kissy noises. The other one walked by everything, but when Mark tried to lead him, he wouldn't go and tried to bite him.

"He's never done that before," the owner said, getting between Mark and the donkey.

Trish faced us and said, "Sparky is our donkey. Please have him here Sunday afternoon for a rehearsal. If everything goes well, he'll only have to come every night the week before Christmas."

"I can do that. I'm glad he'll work out for you." I led Sparky back to the van and loaded him up. Cocoa peered at me over the seat.

"We're going home for lunch and then I have some people to visit." I closed the van doors and heard my name called. Pivoting toward the sound, I spotted Monica. She was the one who suggested Trish call me for the donkey.

"I'm surprised you're not at school," I said when she stopped on the sidewalk near the van.

"It's my prep period. I came over to see if there

was anything else Trish needed help with. How'd Sparky's audition go?"

"He got the part." I made a face. "I didn't realize I'd have to bring him here so many times, but it's for a good cause."

"If you want, Rudy and I can bring him a couple of times. We're in the nativity scene." She smiled and her cheeks blushed.

"Oh, that would be nice. I'll see how things are going by then." I started to ask her if she and Rudy did anything fun last night, and she said, "I have to go. Thanks!"

I waved and slid into the van. "I guess I'll call Rudy. Though if he'd found out anything last night, he would have called me. I bet they didn't get that dinner date with Kyle's friend." Driving out of the parking lot, I headed for home. Sparky didn't need to be cooped up in the van any longer, and I needed nourishment and a plan of action.

Chapter Fourteen

After lunch, I headed back to town with the three dogs. Walking them cleared my brain and it gave me a way to chat with people. I had four people on my list that I wanted to talk to. Two of them worked in the downtown area, one I'd have to go to their farm, and the other was a crafter who worked out of her home.

I decided to take the dogs for a walk at the park and then work our way to the two businesses. As I parked the van, a familiar pickup pulled in behind me. Pretending I didn't see it, I exited the van and walked around to the sliding door.

Sheriff Skala met me there. "I'd think out where you live there would be enough land to walk your dogs."

I smiled and unhooked Cocoa from the seat restraint and hooked her to the leash. She jumped out. I did the same to Lulu and then lifted her out. Then I leaned in, unhooked Athena, and she jumped out, pushing her head against the sheriff's thigh.

"We do have plenty of land, but my dogs like coming to town." I smiled, clicked on my fanny pack, and slid the door closed.

"Are you sure you aren't here to harass more people?" Sheriff Skala fell into step beside me as the dogs wandered along sniffing the grass.

I spun toward him. "I don't harass people. If they are uncomfortable with the questions I ask, then maybe you should be looking at them, not me." Before I could stop myself, I asked, "Who said I'm harassing them?"

Sheriff Skala shook his head. "Stop questioning people and let me and my staff do our job."

"But are you doing your job? I haven't seen you around asking questions."

Sheriff Skala put a hand on my arm. "This isn't a game. You can't go around asking questions. You aren't trained to investigate and interview people."

"I'm being discreet. Well, as discreet as I can when I have to ask blunt questions to get answers." I watched Athena sniffing at the base of a tree and shifted my gaze to Sheriff Skala. "Did Sheila tell you she saw Viola Stevens entering the pavilion as she left after seeing Kyle and Lauren making out?"

He stopped and faced me. "No, she left that out. Is she, and you, insinuating that Viola saw her husband kissing another woman?"

I nodded. "To make sure she wasn't just trying to throw me off her and her husband, I found out which vendors were set up around the Santa area. I plan to ask them if they remember seeing Viola."

"Why don't you give me that information, and we can make inquiries." Sheriff Skala pulled out his notebook.

I reluctantly told him the names, but I wasn't going to tell him where to find them. I planned to talk to them before he did. My conscience battled in my head. I made a pained noise and said, "You should also know that Waldo Dennis made some interesting comments about Lauren." I went on to tell him what Tom and Sheila had said about Waldo and his disillusionment with Lauren. Sighing, I said, "And I suppose Sheila didn't tell you that Lauren told her to take back her man, she didn't want him anymore."

Sheriff Skala's brown eyes studied me. "Lauren told Sheila she was sleeping with her husband?" He shook his head. "I'm really surprised something hadn't happened to that woman sooner."

"You and every other person I've talked to." I bit my tongue, realizing I'd said more than I should have.

Sheriff Skala tipped his head and said, "Tell me more about what Sheila had to say about the victim."

The dogs were pulling on the leashes. I started walking and talking. "Sheila said she believed it was just the woman trying to get to her because Tom would never do that. When I talked to Tom, he said he didn't and would never stray from Sheila." I shrugged. "But who knows if they aren't both saying that to cover for themselves or their spouse."

"You are remarkable in how little you trust people to tell the truth."

I glanced over, watching Sheriff Skala write in his book as we walked.

He glanced up at me. "Did someone in your life lie to you so badly that you don't trust anyone? Your husband, maybe?"

"No, not Mick. He told me everything. Sometimes more than he should have. Growing up with my big sister idolizing someone whom I knew was cruel, talked behind people's backs, and treated her best friend like dirt, I learned to wait until someone proved themselves loyal or truthful before I believed anything."

"You're talking about Viola Stevens." Sheriff Skala closed his notebook. "You don't believe anything she says. What about her husband?"

I stopped and studied him. "Do you really want to know, or are you just going to tell me I need to stop talking to people?"

"I've found your insights on the people involved in this homicide interesting."

He seemed to be telling the truth. Maybe he was coming around to seeing I might be an asset. "At first, I felt sorry for him being married to Viola. But as I talked to him and then some things that Sheila said, I'm wondering if he isn't just as bad as his wife." Nina would never speak to me again if she knew that's what I thought of her best friend and her husband.

"And you believe Sheila and Tom?" Sheriff Skala asked.

I winced. "Not everything they told me, but more than Viola and Kyle."

Sheriff Skala took Athena's leash from me, and we walked back toward the van. "While all of this is good information and I'll check up on it, you need to leave this to my department."

"I have only second-hand information." Which made me consider talking to Waldo and letting the sheriff talk to the vendors.

"I'll get locations on these vendors and see that

Deputy Harper talks to them."

"Is there any evidence to rule out some of the suspects?" I asked, forgetting I had sort of agreed to not be involved anymore. Or at least that's what I wanted him to think.

Sheriff Skala stared at me. "Are you going to let this go?"

I had never been prone to lying. "No. I want justice for Ava and her dad. I want the person who took Lauren away from Ava to get what they deserve."

"I don't like civilians getting caught up in a crime like this." He stared at me and then heaved a weary sigh. "But it might be better if I know what you're doing to keep you safe."

I did a happy dance inside that he might finally be letting me into the investigation and sharing what he knew.

"Do you have any fingerprints to compare to your suspects?" I asked.

"They haven't been able to pick up any fingerprints, which means it was either planned out or the person had on gloves. It *was* cold that evening."

I reached into my memory for the image of Kyle walking out of the community center. He didn't have gloves on. "Sheila said there was a string of lights around Lauren's neck. Was that what killed her?"

"That's information we aren't letting out to the public." The sheriff puffed up like an angry porcupine.

I stopped at the van and faced Sheriff Skala. "Were the lights plugged in? How was it that the tree didn't light? Had the lights been on the tree? Or were they extras, from…?"

"Whoa, that's a lot of questions we've been

working on. Bailey has been talking with the city crew who strung the lights on the tree. Any strands of lights that weren't on the tree went back to the city storage. The one around her neck appeared to have been grabbed off the tree and wrapped around her neck. The reason the tree didn't light was that during the struggle, the lights became unplugged from the main power source." He motioned for me to unlock the doors.

I dug in my fanny pack, pulled out the keys, and unlocked the doors.

He slid the side door open and unhooked Athena so she could jump in. I settled Lulu in the middle, and Cocoa hopped in.

"I'm going to talk to Waldo," I blurted, feeling I needed to keep him in the loop since he just gave me all the information about the murder.

Sheriff Skala studied me. "If I tell you not to, you will anyway, won't you?"

I nodded.

"I can't see you talking to him to be a threat. Be careful and don't say you are helping the police, because you aren't. You're a nosey civilian who won't stay out of our business." He stopped petting Athena and peered into my eyes. "Let me know what you learn or think. I'll round up Bailey, and we'll chase down these vendors and talk to them." He patted Cocoa on the head and walked toward his vehicle.

I watched until he reached the vehicle. Not wanting him to see me watching him, I slid the door closed and walked around to the driver's side. He pulled away from the curb and drove by, giving me a raised hand wave.

My stomach did a little flip, and I chastised myself

for even thinking that man was interesting. Mick had only been gone two years. I didn't need another man in my life so soon. I was finding my stride with my family and therapy animals.

❊ ❊ ❊

The high school parking lot was full. I glanced at the clock in my van and saw it was only 2:17. School didn't get out until 3:30. Did I wait to talk to Waldo after school or go in and see if I could talk to him now? I was here. I might as well see if he was available.

Twisting in my seat to check on the dogs, they were all three staring at the building. "You aren't working here today. Curl up and take a nap, it should be quiet. I parked at the far end of the lot." I slipped out of the van, locked the doors, and strode to the entrance. It was a new building. The one I'd attended had been knocked down, and this one was built in its place.

As I entered, a woman was sitting behind a window similar to what I saw at the Sheriff's Office. She waved me over. "Can I help you?"

"I'd like to talk to the principal, Waldo Dennis." The expression that crossed her face reminded me of an insolent teenager. This woman was in her fifties.

"He took this week off." Her tone said she thought it was a bad idea.

"I didn't know principals could take time off during the school year." I was shocked. When I was in school, the principal was always there keeping an eye on things.

"In all his years as principal, he's never taken even a sick day. But wham! The worst-liked teacher in this school is killed, and he can't come to work." She

123

opened the sliding window farther and leaned out. "I think he's grieving. This is worse than when his wife died. He only took off the day of the funeral, then."

I decided to pretend I liked gossip. "So, were he and the dead teacher involved?"

She shook her head. "He tried to get her interested in him, but she only wanted men who could get in trouble by being with her."

I peered at her like I didn't understand.

"You know, she only went for married men or those in long-term relationships. She liked to stick it to the women, too. I heard her telling one of our staff that her husband would be better in bed if she," the woman blushed, "Well, I can't repeat it, but it had to do with sex." She whispered the last word.

"How many of the teachers' husbands had she slept with, or did she just say that to cause trouble?" I asked, wondering how she could have gotten around to so many men without someone doing something about it sooner.

"I know of two for sure that still work here. Waldo wouldn't fire her, so the other teachers would move."

"Wasn't it hard to find replacement teachers?" I didn't understand how Waldo let Lauren rule his school.

"You know bullies get what they want one way or another."

A woman walked into the office.

"He's not here today. Try back tomorrow," the woman behind the window said and closed it on me.

Chapter Fifteen

I called Mom to find out where Waldo lived. She asked me how things were going. I could hear the spinning wheel in the background, so I just said I was still talking to people.

The modest house on Pine Street was cute with a well-manicured yard and flower beds. I parked in the driveway. There wasn't a car in sight but given the well-kept yard, I imagined the car was in the garage.

"I'll try not to be too long. After this, you can have a pup cup." The dogs' ears popped up at those two words. I slid out, locked the doors, and walked to the front door. Pressing on the doorbell, I listened for sounds from the inside.

It was quiet. No music or television. I pressed the button again, and after several minutes of not hearing anyone coming to the door, I knocked loudly.

The shuffle of slippers grew louder on the other side. I pushed away from where I'd been listening at the door and it opened. Waldo was a mess. Long hair that was most likely usually combed over the top hung down over his right ear, nearly touching his shoulder. His round face was blotchy, his eyes puffy, and he wore a tattered blue and green checked robe and gray, worn slippers.

"Waldo?" I asked.

"Who are you?" he asked, peering at me as if he needed glasses to see.

"I'm Andi Clark. Gina Weber's daughter. I was wondering if I could come in and ask you a few questions about your argument with Lauren and Kyle on Saturday."

His eyes widened. "How do you know about that?"

"Your sister told me. I'm trying to figure out who would have wanted Lauren dead." I pulled on the screen door and it opened.

He turned and headed through the living room. "Come on. Someone needs to know the truth."

I stepped through the doorway and closed both doors before following him into the kitchen. It was small, tidy, and cheerful with a white, red, and black chicken motif. Chicklet would have approved.

"I was just making a pot of coffee. You want some?" He held up an empty coffee pot.

"Yes, I could use a cup. I went to the school first. They told me you weren't coming in all week. Do you think they can function without you for that long?" I didn't really know what a principal did, but they always seemed to be everywhere when I was in school.

"They'll get along fine now that the troublemaker is gone." He turned from filling the pot with water. His face had darkened underneath the splotches.

"You mean Lauren?" I asked.

"I'm sure you have heard all about her from everyone in town. She wasn't a well-liked woman. Even the men she slept with hated her when she was through with them." He poured the water into the coffeemaker and spooned grounds into the filter.

With his body turned as it was, I couldn't see his face to judge his feelings as he talked.

"You talked to some of the men she used?"

He sat down across from me as the coffeemaker started gurgling. "Two male teachers at the school who thought I could do something. Every once in a while, I run into a parent and he seems to feel he can tell me this because I was her boss, I guess."

I studied him. He didn't seem remorseful or angry. He had the look of a trod-upon man who was accepting his fate. "Do you think any of the men you've spoken with would have been so angry as to kill her?"

He shook his head. "They didn't like how things ended, with her blabbing to their wives, but they weren't so angry they'd kill her. That takes a lot of rage."

"Do you know anyone who had that much rage against her?" My mind went to Kyle.

"The guy who was Santa, maybe. When I arrived to give them a piece of my mind, they were quarreling. He said something about 'this was just a fling.' Then she said, 'but it could be so much more now.'" He shoved the long hair that must have tickled his ear with his right hand and smoothed it over the top of his bald head.

My mind raced to the ramifications of these two sentences. It appeared he arrived after Lauren received the call from Nick about the divorce. Which meant she was trying to get Kyle to leave Viola. From the sound of it, he wasn't about to leave his wife and spoil her perfect family reputation.

Waldo rose and filled two cups with coffee. He set one in front of me and slid a sugar bowl in my direction.

"I'm good," I said, trying to figure out what to ask next. "Do you know if Tom ever messed around with Lauren?"

His gaze moved from where he was stirring sugar into his coffee to my face. His eyes were wide. "Tom? He'd never do that to Sheila. Those two have been sweet on each other since high school. He might sound like a tyrant the way he bosses her around, but she wouldn't run around and do his bidding if it were anyone else. They've been like that since they first met. It was Sheila's idea to work in the mayor's office with him. He would have been content for her to stay home and enjoy an early retirement."

"Why do you think Lauren told Sheila that Tom had been a conquest?" I cringed at the old-fashioned word.

"To make her go away, most likely. That seemed to be Lauren's strategy. Say something hurtful and people would leave her alone." He shuttered his eyes as if he didn't want me to see some emotion he was feeling.

"Can you think of any wives who might have hated Lauren enough to get rid of her?" I sipped the almost as good as the Bow Wow Brew's coffee.

"The only one that I can think of with a temper and who would feel like she was being bested, would be Viola Stevens. I didn't know Mr. Stevens, he rarely came to school functions, but when the Stevens children were in school, Viola was the Queen of the PTA and the Athletic Club. She ran things her way, and God help anyone who disagreed with her." He sipped his coffee.

I leaned back in my chair and thought about that. She would be one angry woman to have found out her husband was playing around with the local barracuda.

❊ ❊ ❊

Even though I'd had too much coffee for one day, we stopped at the Bow Wow Brew for the pup cups I'd promised the crew. As we sat on the patio, me spreading the cups around, a county car parked behind my van. I watched Bailey get out, straighten her duty belt, and walk into the patio.

"How's the investigation going?" I asked.

She grinned and said, "I'd think you'd know as much time as the sheriff has been spending with you."

I frowned. "What do you mean?"

"Every time he talks to me asking what I've learned, he gives me a task that he came up with while talking to you." Bailey walked over to the window and ordered. She stood there waiting for the drink before walking over and sitting on the bench across from me. She petted the dogs as they each walked over to sniff and say 'Hi.'

"What did you learn today, then?" I asked, knowing that Sheriff Skala had sent her to talk to vendors. But I didn't want her to put more into him and me talking than she already was.

"The vendors I talked to said they heard a lot of

arguing going on by the Santa sleigh when there weren't kids lined up. Mrs. Perez said Viola walked up to the pavilion with a silly smile on her face, and less than two minutes later, she stormed off with steam coming out her ears." Bailey raised her eyebrows, and I smiled.

"What made her remember seeing Viola?" I asked.

"Because Mrs. Perez had kids the same age as Viola and Kyle's. She said the whole time she saw the woman around the school and at events, she always looked like she was ready to bite someone's head off. When she saw her with a goofy smile, she couldn't believe her eyes, so she watched her until she couldn't see her." Bailey laughed. "Mrs. Perez said that when Viola stormed back by her booth, she looked like the angry woman she remembered and wondered why she was so mad after seeing Santa."

"Because she either came upon her man and his mistress making out, or she heard Lauren telling Kyle to leave his wife." I tossed the last crunchy cone to Athena and wiped my hands. "What time of day was this?"

Bailey stopped slurping on her drink and stared at me. "She said around noon. Where did you hear all of this?"

"I just saw Waldo Dennis. He is one sad man. I don't think he killed Lauren. It's not in him. He did go to have it out with her and heard the conversation between Kyle and Lauren where he said it was only a fling and she said he could get a divorce." I stood. "You can share that with your boss and tell him where it came from. He'll probably want to take down Waldo's statement." I gathered up the leashes and said, "You don't want to tell your mom that her best friend is under suspicion of murder. She's already not talking to me because I didn't answer fast enough when she asked me if I thought Viola did it."

"Copy," Bailey said, also standing and throwing her empty cup in the trash.

"Talk to you soon." I led my dogs to the van and was happy to be going home. This had been an interesting and disturbing day. I'd found good leads for the police to follow, but I'd also learned I needed to keep my interactions with Sheriff Skala less frequent. I needed to think about this and perhaps discuss it with my therapy animals.

Chapter Sixteen

Relaxing on my couch, reading a book, and sipping tea, I heard the crunch of tires on the gravel driveway. Rarely does someone other than family visit and they usually walk over. Athena and Cocoa's heads raised and their ears cocked. Lulu jumped off the couch where she'd been lying beside me and started barking her sharp intruder bark.

"Tone it down," I said, pulling the belt on my robe tighter and walking to the door.

There was a knock and the door opened. Rudy let himself in and strode over to the propane fireplace in the corner of the room. "It's cold out tonight," he said.

"Is that why you drove the quarter mile from your place to mine?" I asked sarcastically.

"Ha ha, very funny. No, I came from town and dinner with Monica. We met Carson and his wife. You know, Kyle's friend?"

"I'm impressed you managed to have dinner with

him and that you are home this early from a date with Monica." I motioned to the kitchen. "Want something warm to drink?"

"Yeah, hot chocolate and Bailey's, please. I'll stand here and get warm while you make it." He grinned and I felt like the big sister whom he always came to when he was in trouble.

"Is there more to this meeting than you're letting on?" I asked, walking into the kitchen. As I figured, he followed me.

"Yeah." He pulled out a chair at the table and sat. "The dinner was going well until I brought up Lauren. Carson's wife became angry, and Monica asked me what I was doing. I said I was just wondering if Kyle and Lauren were going at it."

I turned from putting the mug of milk in the microwave and stared at him. "Did you use those words?" I couldn't believe how uncouth he'd been.

He ducked his head, "Yeah, you know, we guys talk like that to each other. I figured Carson would think of me as one of his friends, but he even looked at me as if I shouldn't be at the table with them."

"You were supposed to be subtle, not go in like a bulldozer. Sheesh, now I probably won't be able to talk to him." The microwave dinged. I pulled the milk out, added the hot chocolate mix, stirred, and added the Bailey's. "I see why you need this." I set the drink in front of him. "Want to talk here or sit in the living room?"

"In there, it's warmer and more comfortable chairs." He picked up his drink and stood, walking into the living room and sitting on the opposite end of the couch from where I'd been reading.

Cocoa walked over and put her head in his lap, and Athena stood beside the arm of the couch, peering up at him. Lulu had been curled up in the middle of the couch. She stretched and lay across Rudy's lap. They felt his sorrow.

"Yeah, the meal was pretty quiet after that." He sipped his drink and stared at the fire. "But afterward, when I took Monica home, she said it was insensitive because of the way I said it and because Carson's wife had been one of the women that Lauren told she was having an affair with her husband. Carson denied it and told her it was Kyle who Lauren was sleeping with, not him."

I leaned toward him. "So, he did know about Kyle and Lauren. Maybe I could visit with him when his wife isn't around. I would say he wouldn't want to talk about the woman at all around her."

"Yeah, Monica said, I should have waited until the women went to the restroom to ask him." He ran a hand over his face. "I didn't know there was so much to learn about this detecting."

I chuckled. "You've always had a lack of decorum. But I'm glad you were willing to help."

We sat in silence sipping our drinks, and I asked, "Where does Carson work?"

"He's the manager at the Community Bank." Rudy studied me. "Are you going to talk to him?"

"Not at the bank. Do you know anything else about him?" I didn't want to walk into the bank and start asking him about his philandering friend.

"I'll text Monica to call or text you what she knows about his life outside of work. That way she knows I won't be the insensitive oaf talking to him." He pulled out his phone and typed.

A few minutes later my phone dinged in the kitchen, where it was charging on the counter. I tend to leave it overnight in the kitchen charging. That way it's always ready the next day. I rose off the couch and walked into the room. Monica had texted me.

I'm glad it's you who is going to talk to him. I know Rudy thought he was helping, but he really isn't the right person to send to interview anyone.

I was worried about it when he mentioned talking to Carson. I texted back.

She sent me a cringing face emoji and texted, *Carson is a coach for the parks and rec. He has practices or games every day at 4. If you don't want to catch him there, he works out at the YMCA every morning at 6:30.*

Thank you, I texted back.

"Was that Monica?" Rudy asked as I returned to the couch.

"Yes. I'll go talk to Carson tomorrow. You just listen and don't ask people questions."

Rudy frowned. "That's the same thing Monica said."

"Finish your drink and go home. I have to get up early tomorrow." I finished off my tea, and he downed the rest of his drink. "In the morning, if I'm not back when you're helping David with the chores, could you let these three out to do their business? I'll be back by nine. We have to be at Rockin' Retirement at ten."

"Yeah, I'll check on the mutts." He patted all their heads and moved Lulu off his lap. "I hope you have better luck than I did."

As I held the door open for him, I said, "It's all in

the delivery."

He stopped and studied me. "How do you know so much about interrogating people?"

"It's not interrogating, it's asking them questions that lead them to tell you more. Mick taught me. I'd go along when he was looking into discrepancies. He had a knack for asking the questions that helped him find the missing or hidden money." To myself I thought *or the bodies*.

"I didn't realize that was what he did. I just knew he helped advise people about money. Huh?" He stepped out the door, zipping up his coat. "Thanks for warming me up and not chewing me out for screwing up."

"You'll get the hang of it." I closed the door and hoped we didn't have to help find a killer again anytime soon.

"Looks like you guys can sleep in tomorrow while I go check out the YMCA." I turned off the lights, and everyone followed me into the bedroom. Cocoa and Athena settled on their dog beds on the floor. Lulu used the stairs onto my bed to curl up in her cave bed on Mick's side.

I didn't want a large dog in bed with me, but having Lulu breathing on that side of the bed made me feel safe. As if it were Mick still sleeping beside me. Though he didn't snore like Lulu.

After brushing my teeth and setting out workout clothes, I slid into bed and turned out the light. Five-thirty was going to come way too soon.

Chapter Seventeen

My van windows were frosted when I went out at six to leave for the YMCA. I started the van, directing all the cold, and hopefully soon, warm air on the front windshield. Back in the house waiting for the window to clear, I ate a granola bar and drank another cup of coffee. The dogs looked at me as if I were a stranger. It was rare anymore that I got out of bed before seven. I had no reason to get up earlier than that. All the things I did were set at times later in the day.

I hadn't mentioned to Rudy to feed Cupcake, Sparky, Chicklet, Flopsie, and the other small animals, but I knew he would while the dogs were out running around doing their business. I'd check on them to be sure when I returned home.

I glanced out the living room window and saw a clear spot large enough that I could see to get out to the county road. After that, the rest should thaw quickly.

"You three be good. Rudy will let you out at your

usual time. See you before nine." I patted their heads and walked out the door, remembering to lock it.

In the van, the air blowing was warm, not hot, but it was enough to get the windows thawing. I turned on the wipers and scraped away more of the loosened frost. Driving to town was slow. The road appeared frosty in spots. I stayed at a responsible speed even though two vehicles roared around me.

At the YMCA, I walked in and over to the sign-in counter. "Hi, I'd like to sign up to be a member."

The young man in his twenties, with a sleeveless shirt that showed off muscled arms, smiled at me. "I'm Ethan."

"Andi. I moved back a year ago but have just now figured out a schedule to be able to come in regularly."

"Fill out this paper. It's just saying you won't find us liable for any injuries you may incur while working out here." He smiled and handed me a clipboard with a form.

"Okay. Do many people get injured?"

"Only if they are using the equipment wrong or are goofing around. I don't see that being a problem for you." Ethan smiled again and handed me another paper. "This is your information and who to call if you should require medical assistance."

I stared at him. "You're sure this place is safe?"

"It's just a precaution. You know, with so many people wanting to sue." He shrugged.

It wasn't his fault that all these papers had to be signed, however, it made me wonder if exercising was that good for a person. "Sorry to be a complainer. Will someone give me a tour of the facilities?" I signed the first paper and quickly filled in the information on the second one.

"Yeah, I will." He smiled, took the papers, and handed me a lanyard with a card that said member.

"Do I have to wear this while I'm sweating?" I asked, pulling it over my head.

"No. You only need it when you come in. The card gets you into the locker room and out to the machines."

He led me to a door to the right of the glass wall, revealing all kinds of torture machines and people using them. "This is the women's locker room. Go ahead and store your stuff and come out onto the exercise floor. I'll meet you there." He left and I ducked into the locker room.

Two women were talking and changing into workout clothes. I smiled, studied the lockers, and saw they had combination locks.

"Excuse me, how do these work?" I asked.

One of the women came over and showed me how to set the combination on my own.

"Do I do this every time I come in?" I asked, thinking that was good and bad.

"Yes. You'll get the hang of it," the woman said, picking up a water bottle and following her friend out of the area.

I mumbled and set the lock after putting my fanny pack, boots, and coat in the locker. I came in my workout clothes. Now to find Carson. I'd looked him up on the bank's website and found a photo of him. I didn't want to wander around the place asking each man if he was Carson or ask to have him pointed out to me. I planned to walk up to him like I knew him. Hoping he'd think I was one of his wife's friends or a client of the bank.

I pushed through the door. Ethan was chatting with, of all people, Carson. "I didn't know you worked out here this early in the morning," I said, walking up and smiling at Carson.

His forehead wrinkled, but he smiled and replied, "Yeah, every weekday before work."

"Nice."

Ethan smiled. "Carson, since you know Andi, why don't you show her around, and I can get back to the front desk."

"That would be great." I smiled at Carson and added, "If you have the time." I could tell he was still trying to place me.

"Sure, why not? It saves me from having to do more crunches." He waved a hand for me to move along to the first machine. We walked over and Carson pointed out the poster showing what to do on each machine and what muscle groups it worked. "You might want someone knowledgeable to go around with you the first couple of times to make sure you aren't using the wrong muscles. That can end up hurting something."

I faced him and said, "Now I'm really worried. I had to sign a form saying this place wasn't liable for any injuries incurred and now you are saying I could get hurt if I don't know what I'm doing. I'm beginning to wonder if this is right for me."

"No, I'm just saying you can hurt yourself by not using the machine correctly. Hurt as in making muscles sore that shouldn't be sore. Not to the point you'd need a doctor or anything like that." He moved on to the next machine.

In the extras room, where a person could grab a

jump rope, medicine ball, kettlebell, stability ball, or ropes, I picked up a jump rope and asked, "What can you tell me about Lauren and Kyle?"

He stopped bending to reach for a kettlebell and straightened. His face was set in a scowl. "What are you, a reporter or something?"

I smiled and shook my head. "Nope. Just someone helping to discover who killed Lauren so the community can get back to normal."

"Kyle didn't kill her." He studied me. "Who are you giving this information to?"

"The sheriff."

"Are you a detective with the Sheriff's Department?" he asked.

I chuckled and said, "No, a concerned citizen who didn't know the victim. She wasn't a nice person, and there are lots of people who had reason to want her killed, but I'm looking for the one who stood to lose the most if she stayed alive." I peered into his hazel eyes, hoping he took the bait.

"Sheriff Skala has you interviewing people? That's crazy. That doesn't sound like the Jason I know. He would come and talk to me himself."

I didn't realize he knew Sheriff Skala. "I came across your name as someone who could give me some information about Kyle and Lauren. I hadn't told Jason yet." I shrugged. "If you feel more comfortable talking to him, I'm okay with that." And I was. If he and Sheriff Skala were friends, I would rather have Carson rat out Kyle or Viola to him than me, then I wouldn't have to take the news to Jason.

"No, if he sent you to dig around, I'm good with that." He nodded to the door. "Too many ears here. Did you really come here to work out or to talk to me?"

My cheeks heated. "Just to talk to you. I get a good enough workout on the farm with my animals."

"Ok. I'll go change and meet you at J&P Bakery in fifteen minutes."

I stared at him. "You think there will be more privacy there? Everyone will be in there getting their morning latte and donuts."

"True, but I need breakfast."

"Let's meet at Heidi's Kitchen. We can get a quiet booth in the corner and see who is around us before talking." Not that this was some clandestine meeting between spies, but there were a lot of big ears and even bigger mouths in this town.

"I'll meet you there." He left the room, and I dropped the jump rope and headed to the locker room to gather my things. As I left the building, Ethan called out. "You didn't stay very long."

"I remembered a business meeting I have to get to. I'll try for tomorrow." I smiled, walking to the van. I didn't plan to set foot in there again if I could help it.

At Heidi's, I didn't see Carson. I asked for a table in the corner. Sipping my coffee, I was wondering if he'd ditched me when Carson walked into the restaurant with a woman.

I waved and he nodded, maneuvering the woman to the corner with his hand on her back. Once they were seated, Carson made the introductions. "Andi, this is my wife, Carla. I brought her along to make sure no rumors start flying about us and so Carla can verify and remind me of things."

I smiled at the pretty blonde with streaks of gray in her hair as we shook hands over the table.

"Are you Nina Harper's sister?" she asked.

"I am, but please don't hold that against me."

She chuckled. "I heard that you two were as different as night and day, and I can already see that. You do know that if she or Viola hears about this, you could be in for trouble."

I waved my hand. "Those two have always had it out for me and I never knew why. I don't care who is friends with whom. I want to find the killer and make everyone feel safe again."

Carla looked confused. "I thought you were working for Jason?"

"I'm helping him, but I also want to help the town." I picked up a menu. "Shall we order before we start talking so you can get to work on time?"

They conceded, and the waitress took our order. When she left, I asked, "Was Kyle actually contemplating leaving Viola for Lauren or was he just having a fling?"

Carson glanced at his wife and said, "He was just having a fling. In case you haven't noticed, Viola isn't all that cuddly. A man needs a woman to hold and be held by now and then."

"But Lauren? Surely, he could have found someone less like his wife than her? From what I've heard, she was as cold-hearted and ruthless as Viola." I didn't see how someone as calculating as Lauren could lure men in like she did.

"You didn't hear this from me, but most of the men who really slept with Lauren did it because it was something more interesting than their wives." Carson glanced at his wife and they shared an intimate moment like what Mick and I had many times during our marriage. I was positive Carson hadn't been one of Lauren's conquests and would hopefully give us the answers we needed.

"From what you're saying, Lauren confessed to sleeping with many more men than she actually did?"

Carson nodded. "Like her telling Carla that she'd slept with me. There is no way I would have even thought of that. I'm in love with my wife. I've talked to other men whom Lauren had told wives she'd slept with their husbands and she hadn't."

"It was her deflection method, just like Waldo said." I thought about that. "Do you know the men she did sleep with? That would narrow the pool of suspects unless some of the wives believed her and not their husbands." I ran my finger up and down the handle of the knife in front of me.

The waitress arrived with our breakfast. Mine was eggs, toast, and bacon. Carson had a plate piled with an omelet, hashbrowns, and toast. Carla had fruit and oatmeal.

As we dug in, I asked the questions I'd been holding back. "Do you think Kyle was thinking about leaving Viola for Lauren?"

They both stopped eating and peered at me. Carson shook his head. "He may not be in a marriage full of love, but he wouldn't leave Viola. She would turn the kids against him and he couldn't take that. And he would lose everything. Viola owns the real estate business. He came into it after he got in a fight with his dad and was kicked out of the family business."

"Okay. My next question is, would he kill to not lose everything?" I saw they were pondering this longer than someone who was certain a person wouldn't commit a crime.

Carson shook his head. "The man I knew growing up wouldn't hurt anything. He liked baseball because it was, for the most part, a noncontact sport. He couldn't stomach hurting anyone. But the longer he's lived with Viola, the more cutthroat he's become."

Carla nodded her head. "I agree. The older he gets and the longer he's with Viola, he's become more bitter and hardened. I couldn't believe it when Carson told me he had hooked up with Lauren. Like you, I would have thought he'd have found a more nurturing woman."

"Let's switch this up. Do you know if Viola knew about Kyle and Lauren?" My money was on Viola choking Lauren with Christmas lights.

"If she had known, I would have heard about it," Carson said.

Nodding, Carla said, "Yes, I think Lauren was smart enough or scared enough of Viola to keep her mouth shut this time."

I finished my breakfast and said, "I'll pass what you said along to Jason. He might call you to get official statements, I'm not sure." Then, to satisfy my curiosity, I asked, "How do you two know Jason?"

Carson's eyes dulled. "His wife was my cousin. When she passed, we spent a lot of time helping him deal with Noah, their son. He's the same age as our youngest, eighteen."

My gut twisted, realizing Sheriff Skala had gone through a similar situation to mine. Only he had a child to remind him daily of the woman he missed. All I had were photos of Mick and the few belongings I couldn't give up. "Is his son living with him here in Auburn?" I asked.

"He's been trying to find a job, but if he can't find one here, he'll probably move onto the reservation with his family on Jason's side." Carla sighed. "He has so much potential. He's an artist, but he needs more schooling on technique. That's why he wants a job, to help pay for classes."

"I hope he finds one so he and Jason can stay together." I stood. "I'll get the ticket. Thank you for being honest with me. Of all the people I've talked to so far, you are the first ones I can tell aren't hiding something."

Carla smiled. "Don't worry about your sister and Viola. The rest of the women in this town would be happy to have you join our clubs and circles."

"Thank you. I've never worried about what Nina and Viola thought of me. I think that's what makes them dislike me even more. I can't be bullied or badgered by them." I smiled. "I'm still trying to get my feet under me here, but as soon as I feel solid, I'll contact you and join in."

"We'd love it." Carla and Carson slid out of the booth and walked with me to the cash register.

I paid the bill and we walked out to the sidewalk.

"That's right, you have the therapy animals. Mrs. Bunton at the Rockin' Retirement home said your animals always brighten the residents' day." Carla stared at my van with the Cuddle Farm logo on the side.

"We're headed there today. Every Wednesday at ten. I need to get rolling so I have time to pick up the animals and get there. Again, thank you for talking to me, and it was a pleasure meeting you both."

"Us as well," Carson said, and they strolled down the street arm in arm.

I slid into the van, cranked it over, and headed home. We would be late to the retirement facility if I didn't get home and load everyone up. As I drove, I thought about who might be looking for help and could give Jason's son a job.

Chapter Eighteen

Mrs. Bunton stood at the entrance to Rockin' Retirement facility. She smiled and took the dogs' leashes so I could retrieve Flopsie and Chicklet's cages from the van. In warmer weather, Sparky and Cupcake would join us when we could congregate outside in the sunshine. Today, with the cold wind and the possibility of snow, we would have to stay in the recreation room.

At the rec room, I spotted Lulu already on Roger's lap, getting her belly scratched. Cocoa was sitting between Doris and Shirley, being petted and talked to. Athena stood next to Frank's tilted-back wheelchair. Her head was underneath his hand that dangled over the side of the chair. His fingers moved slightly as if he were petting her. Frank had a stroke two years earlier. Mrs. Bunton told me the first time I brought the animals that Frank hadn't moved more than to stay alive until he touched Athena's head that first visit.

I walked over to the table with a plastic cloth

draped over it. I set the cages on each end and opened the doors. Flopsie hopped out. The residents who wanted to visit with the animals were in the room. Beatrice already had her walker beside the table. She knew the routine. Her hand was extended over the table with a piece of lettuce she must have swiped from the kitchen. Flopsie hopped to her hand and started nibbling. The bunny sat still as Beatrice ran her gnarled hand down the rabbit's soft fur.

Raymond rolled his wheelchair over to Chicklet's cage. He had a newspaper on his lap. He clucked at the hen, and she walked out of the cage. She turned her head back and forth as Raymond clucked, then hopped down into his lap. He stroked her feathers and talked to her.

The dogs wandered from person to person, and residents moved to the table to visit with Chicklet and Flopsie. After ninety minutes, the bell for the residents' lunch sounded.

Those who could talk thanked me and said goodbye to the animals. As I was loading Chicklet into her cage, Shirley walked over. Leaning on her cane, she stood beside the table as I closed the door on Chicklet and reached across the table to pick up Flopsie.

"You know that woman who was killed before the tree lighting?" Shirley asked quietly.

I focused on her, holding Flopsie in my arms. "I didn't know her, but I know what happened, why?"

"Her father is in here. He said she was gloating about having the principal wrapped around her finger and she'd soon be promoted. Do you think the job she was taking over got her killed?" Shirley peered down at me with rheumy eyes and sagging cheeks. Even while bent from osteoporosis, she was taller than my five-seven frame.

"Who is her father?" I asked, thinking this might be something to look into.

"James Roman. I can take you to him. We play cards every afternoon." Color rose on Shirley's cheeks.

"Don't you both need to eat lunch?" I asked.

"He doesn't come out of his room for meals. They take it to him. I can drop you off and get my grub." Shirley pointed at the cages with her cane. "Leave them there. It's warmer in here." Then she motioned to the dogs. "You can bring them. James likes dogs."

"Why didn't he come to see them?" I asked, making sure the cages were closed and the small combination locks were secured. I didn't want one of the residents to wander in and let them out.

"He prefers to stay in his room. Too many rumors about his daughter out here in the public."

I gathered the dogs' leashes and walked beside Shirley as we shuffled down the hall.

"Shirley, where are you taking Andi and her dogs?" Mrs. Bunton asked as she turned the corner coming toward us.

"To see James. He likes dogs." Shirley smiled at the other woman.

Mrs. Bunton shifted her gaze to me. "Where are the cages?"

"Still on the table. I locked them so no one could get Flopsie or Chicklet out. I'll only stay fifteen minutes and then get them out of your way," I said.

"Stay as long as James needs. He lost a daughter this week." Mrs. Bunton started to leave, then added, "Shirley, you show Andi to the room and then go to the dining room and eat your lunch."

"I will," Shirley said, smiling and waving her cane at Mrs. Bunton. When the woman had disappeared, Shirley said, "She works hard and sounds harsh, but if you had to yell most of the day to make people hear you, you'd sound harsh too."

I agreed with her, and she knocked on a closed door.

"James, it's Shirley. I have a surprise." She opened the door. The dogs all moved into the room ahead of me.

The short, round man in the recliner came to life at the sight of the dogs. "Who are you?" he asked, ruffling Cocoa and Athena's ears as Lulu jumped up in his lap.

I introduced the dogs to him and settled into the hardback chair I found by the door.

"I'm going to lunch," Shirley said, stopping at the table near his chair. "You need to eat this when you finish petting the dogs." She gave him a stern look. As she passed by me, she said, "You have to treat men like little boys at this age." She winked and left the room.

"Are these your dogs?" James asked.

"Yes, they are. We come every Wednesday to Rockin' to visit. If you come down to the rec room at ten, you can see us every week," I offered.

"They're beautiful dogs. Just beautiful. I had a dog when I was a child. I loved that mutt. He lasted until I was seventeen. Died of old age and I nearly died of a broken heart. My parents wouldn't let me get another one because I'd be leaving home soon. I joined the Army and then got married. After that, I never seemed to have time for a dog. When we had a daughter, I got her a puppy. But when I paid it more attention than her, she hurt it, so I gave it to a deserving little boy." His eyes watered and drops fell on Lulu's head.

I wondered if he was sad for the dog or his daughter. "I was sorry to hear about Lauren," I said, to get to the subject I wanted to ask.

He nodded, the tears still falling. "You never want to outlive your children. It's lonely."

Not having children, I'd never thought about it being lonely as I grew old. I had all my family, but two of them were older than me. I could be alone at the end. My gaze wandered to my dogs. I knew I would never be alone as long as I had animals in my life.

"Can you tell me about her, or is that too painful?" I asked.

"No, I like to talk about her. She was a teacher. She'd always wanted to be a teacher since she was in elementary school. When she moved here after college, I was surprised. She always talked about living in a big city. But I think she couldn't get into the larger schools. She wasn't the best student. Her mother was always getting called into school because Lauren was in trouble." He frowned.

Athena licked his cheek.

He smiled and patted her head. "You're a good girl, aren't you?"

"Was Lauren happy working at the high school here?" I asked to bring him back to the conversation.

"Yes, she liked it until she started losing friends. I'm not sure what happened. Her letters were full of the friends she was making. After her mother died and she brought me here, she started hating the school, the other teachers, the principal. She didn't have a nice thing to say about anyone. Until last week. She came in with a smile on her face and said that she was nominated for Teacher of the Year and expected to be moved to assistant principal. She said she was the teacher who had been at the high school the longest. The principal had talked to her about the promotion." He glanced up from petting the dogs and said, "She was just getting back to the happy girl I remembered, and now she's gone."

"I'm sorry for your loss." I sat there another ten minutes letting him pet the dogs and talk to them before I said, "I'm sorry, we need to get going. We'll be back next Wednesday if you want to come out to the recreation room at ten." I rose from the chair and grabbed the leashes strewn across the floor around James' chair.

"Yes, these lovely creatures need to go spread their happiness around. Thank you for bringing them in to see me." James tucked his hands on his lap and smiled.

"Don't forget to eat your lunch. Do you want me to bring it over to you?" I asked, reaching out to grab the tray holding what looked like a nourishing lunch.

"I'll get it in a minute. I need to use the can first."

"Okay, have a good rest of your day," I said, letting us out of his room and walking down the hall toward the rec room. His words about Lauren becoming an assistant principal bothered me. Had she made that up or had Waldo promised her that? He hadn't said anything when I talked to him.

I led the dogs out to the van and clipped them in before heading back in for Chicklet and Flopsie. Doris was petting Flopsie with a finger stuck through the cage. "Hi, Doris. I have to take them home now. They'd like to get out of their little cages."

"Yes, let them out. We don't get out of this cage unless family comes and gets us." She watched me pick up the cages. "Do you think they'd let me have a bunny in my room?"

"I don't know. You could ask and see, I guess. It never hurts to ask. See you next week." I walked to the door.

"I hope so," her voice carried down the hall toward me.

I sighed and hoped I would see her next week. During these weekly visits, I'd gotten to know nearly half the residents well and would be sad when their time to leave the earth came.

Chapter Nineteen

As I loaded Chicklet and Flopsie, I decided to have dinner with Rudy and Monica. I could pick Monica's brain about the possibility of Lauren becoming an Assistant Principal.

On the way home, I also realized I needed to update Sheriff Skala on what I'd found out from Carson, Carla, and James. I didn't want to call him, but I was doing all this investigating to help him find the killer. I wasn't the law.

I decided to wait until I had the animals unloaded and snuggled in before I made that call. I texted Rudy as soon as I parked in front of my house.

I want to take you and Monica out for dinner tonight. Can you make that happen?

When and where? He texted back.

6 at Auburn House.

He sent a thumbs-up emoji.

My stomach growled and I realized it was getting close to one. I stepped out, slid the side door open, and unlatched and unharnessed the dogs. All three flew out of the van and started sniffing and squatting. "I'm glad you waited until now."

I went to the back of the van and opened the doors to pull out Chicklet. Sparky started braying. He knew we were home and he would be let out into the small pasture.

Carrying Chicklet to the heated shed where she and three other silky chickens live, I laughed at the antics of the dogs as they chased leaves the wind carried across the ground. Chicklet hopped out of her cage and into the heated coop as her three friends ran in from the outside run. The run was covered with wire and had wire buried three feet in the ground around their 20 x 20 outdoor run.

I carried the cage to my back door and went to the van to get Flopsie. Sparky's braying hadn't let up. It wasn't like him to keep making noise. At the heated building that housed Flopsie's hutch, and that of two of her bunny friends, I let Flopsie loose on the floor. She hopped over to a water bottle and drank before hopping out the door to join her friends in a matching wire-enclosed pen like the chickens. Checking the water and feeders, and seeing that the doors had been opened to the outside areas, I knew that Rudy had taken care of them this morning.

But that didn't seem to matter to Sparky, who was still braying as if he were being kidnapped. I set the rabbit cage in the path to the house and walked to the barn to see why Sparky was making so much noise.

I realized the problem as soon as his pen came into sight. Cupcake was wedged between one of her boxes and the wire panel between her pen and Sparky's.

"How did you manage this, girl?" I asked, opening the gate to her pen and jogging over to where she was stuck. She appeared to have tipped the box against the fence and then decided to get on top of it. She must have fell down between the box and the fence. I'd have to find a way to nail the box down or put a bottom on it and fill it with weight so she didn't do this again.

I pulled the box back, and she trotted out from between it and the fence, circling to come to me. I scratched her neck and head. "You don't look too scared or hurt." When she walked over to touch noses with Sparky, I moved the box to the middle of the pen. She must have been pushing it around for it to have made it over by the fence. I gave her a handful of grain and then took a small portion of grain to Sparky.

"You were a good boy to let me know something was wrong," I said, scratching his neck as he ate the grain.

The dogs started barking and the sound of a vehicle coming down the driveway started my heart pumping.

Lulu!

I ran out of the barn calling to her.

Lulu ran toward me. I'd taught her to come to me when there was a moving vehicle. I leaned down and she jumped into my arms. When my fear abated, I glanced toward the driveway to find Sheriff Skala scratching Athena and Cocoa.

I put Lulu on the ground to run to him and walked over to get the rabbit cage. I had to clean both the cages so they would be ready for our next outing. "What brings you out here?" I asked, walking by the sheriff and around to the back door.

He followed, as did the dogs. "I heard you were

talking to Carson and Carla. Thought you might have something for me."

Stopping, I spun to face him. "How did you know I talked to them?"

"Bailey saw you at Heidi's this morning being cozy with them." He grinned. "They're a good couple to be cozy with."

"You only say that because you're related to them."

"By marriage." He sobered and stared across the field that ran alongside my house.

I softened. "I heard. Sorry for your loss. I know the feeling." I peered into his eyes and felt his grief.

"Well, we have to move on."

When I bent to pick up Chicklet's cage, he grabbed it. "Where are you going with these?"

"I just returned from visiting the retirement home and need to clean them before anything dries on." I opened the back door and set Flopsie's cage on the drainboard in the mudroom. In the corner of the mudroom was a special tub with a flexible shower head where I washed the big dogs. Lulu fit in the sink.

"You have this place set up for all your animals." His voice held respect.

"They were my first priority when I had the plans made." I finished spraying out Chicklet's pen and set it in the dog shower. I took the rabbit cage, dumping the manure from the pan underneath into my compost can, and then cleaned the cage.

Sheriff Skala leaned against the doorjamb into the house until the banging stopped and the water heater beside the sink stopped humming. In the silence that followed, he asked, "Did you learn anything new?"

I set the cage beside the other one in the dog

shower, dried my hands, and nodded to the door into the kitchen. "I'm starving. Do you need lunch?" I walked into the kitchen, washed my hands with soap, and pulled sandwich ingredients from the fridge.

"Are you avoiding my question?" he asked. "And yes, I could eat lunch."

I put the sandwich fixings on the table and then placed a cup of coffee in front of him. "Sheriff—"

He put up a hand to stop me. "Jason. You can call me Sheriff Skala when other people are around."

"Okay, Jason, I'm not avoiding your question. I'm starving and want some food in my stomach so I can remember everything."

He nodded and started making a sandwich on the plate I handed him.

When I had a ham and Swiss on sourdough with pickles and chips made and had eaten half the sandwich, I leaned back and sighed. "Now I can tell you what I learned," I told him what Carson and Carla had to say about both Kyle and Viola. "So they didn't say they couldn't have done it, but they also didn't say they could." I picked up the other half of my sandwich. "At the retirement home, I had an interesting talk with Lauren's father." I took a bite, chewed, swallowed, and said, "He said she was expecting to be promoted to assistant principal."

Jason stopped with the coffee mug halfway to his mouth. "No one else has mentioned this?"

"No. You would have thought that Waldo would have mentioned it." I took another bite and, after I swallowed, said, "I'm having dinner tonight with Rudy and his girlfriend, Monica. She's a teacher at the high school. I was going to ask her some questions about this new development."

He nodded. "Good idea. We need to find out who did this before Saturday. Bailey said a lot of people don't want to go to the tree lighting after what happened last weekend."

I stared at him. "Do you blame them? They don't know what we know about her death."

Jason peered at me with a furrowed brow. "What do we know about her death?"

"That it was a one-time thing. This was definitely a crime of passion and not some rogue person going around killing people." I finished off my sandwich and picked up my cup of coffee.

"How did you come to that conclusion? And how do you know this person won't kill again to keep their secret?" He tossed his napkin on his plate and leaned back, studying me.

"We haven't found any proof that Lauren was blackmailing anyone. We do know that she was sleeping with some men, but not all of the ones that she proclaimed to have slept with. There could be a wife out there who killed Lauren, and that woman's husband hadn't even slept with the victim." I took a sip of coffee and continued. "I can see Waldo as the killer. He's avoiding work and isn't taking care of himself. Lauren seemed to have gotten a lot out of him, yet he received nothing in return except to be dumped on. Crime of passion. He wanted Lauren. All she did was string him along. Now he's ashamed of what he did but too weak to confess." I rose to grab the cookie jar.

"That's thought out, but I don't think he did it. Yes, he was at the Santa area and probably saw and heard what he told you, but at the time of death, he was sitting in Hop On Inn drinking away his sorrows."

"He was at a brewery while his sister and her husband were busy with their biggest community event of the year?" I had expected Waldo to be at the tree lighting. "Where did you get this information?"

"From Darren, he manages the brewpub. I was in there last night getting dinner. He heard I'd been the one to 'not light up the tree.' After the event didn't go as planned, he was glad that he had worked and let others attend. He said the only people in the pub were the principal and two older men who spend most nights in the establishment."

"Did you specifically ask if it was Waldo?" I didn't see him frequenting the Hop on Inn, but then it wouldn't be the first time I had pegged a person wrong.

"Yes, he said about two months ago, Waldo started coming in nearly every night. He sits at the bar, hunched over a drink that he nurses for a couple of hours, and then leaves. Once in a while, someone will stop and talk to him, but he always sits there alone." Jason finished off his coffee and stood. "Come by the office tomorrow morning. We'll go over what you learn from Monica tonight. It will help me decide how to approach Waldo about his not telling us everything."

I nodded, really not wanting to go to the office and have Bailey make more insinuations. "Or we could meet at the Bow Wow Brew at ten?"

His gaze remained on my eyes longer than was necessary. "Why not meet at the office?"

I picked up the dishes and set them in the sink to give myself time to figure out how to form what I wanted to say. Facing him, I said, "Bailey thinks there is something more than professional going on between us. I don't want her seeing me at the office and then telling my family what she said to me."

"You don't want to be linked to me in friendship?" he asked, spinning his hat in his hands.

"No, that's not it. I'm great with a friendship. She was implying it was more and it's not. I told her that, but she just kept smiling. You have to know her better." I was at a loss for words and just shut up.

A smile slowly formed and his eyes lit up. "You want to be friends and nothing more. That's all I thought we were."

I felt like a balloon deflating. He understood. "Exactly, just friends."

"Then coming to the office in an official capacity would be more friendship than us meeting away from the office." He raised an eyebrow.

"Like this, where you came to my house and I fed you lunch." I sighed and collapsed onto the closest chair. "I'll be at your office at ten. Is that early enough?"

"That will work. See you tomorrow." He walked out the back door, and I flopped my head into my hands, feeling like a fool.

Something nudged my elbow. I opened an eye and smiled at Cocoa. "I'm fine. Just feeling stupid. Now Jason thinks I do like him more than as friends. I don't need another man in my life, one was enough." I put my arms around Cocoa and Athena's necks and hugged them. "You are all I need."

Chapter Twenty

Rudy and Monica walked into the Auburn House as the hostess seated me. I waved them over and we ordered drinks.

I enjoyed watching my kid brother, who always seemed like such a goofball, hold Monica's chair when she sat and then make sure she was warm enough.

"Why did you invite us to dinner?" Rudy asked, just as the waitress returned with our drinks.

"Let's figure out what we want to eat first," I said, smiling at the waitress while we made our choices.

When the waitress left with our order, I said, "Monica, what can you tell me about Lauren being made assistant principal?"

Her mouth opened and her eyes widened before she caught herself and stammered, "T-t-that would be impossible. As far as I know, she hasn't been doing any continued training to be qualified for the job."

I ran a finger around the edge of my wine glass. "What you're saying is she wasn't qualified and there would have been uproar had she been given that job." I glanced up at Monica.

"Oh, yeah. I can think of three teachers who are taking the classes to move up to an administrative position. If she had been given that job, I can guarantee that Waldo would be out of a job and anyone else who okayed that position. It was one thing to nominate her for Teacher of the Year. We all knew she would never win. But for her to just be handed a promotion without further training… That would have made a lot of people furious. Not to mention it's the superintendent's job to pick the principal and assistant principal for schools." Monica picked up her wine glass and downed half of it.

"So, you didn't hear about this? And Waldo had no authority to promise Lauren the job?" I wondered if Waldo had only told Lauren that to lure her into going on a date with him.

"No. And I can guarantee if anyone at the school had known, there would have been a protest." Monica swallowed the rest of her wine.

Rudy refilled her glass.

This was one more motive for Waldo to have killed Lauren. If he promised her the job and knew the trouble it would bring to the school and himself, her not following through with whatever her favor was and giving his Santa gig to Kyle, Waldo could have been furious and realized she would never follow through on her end of whatever deal they had. Learning it was the superintendent's job to pick, I wondered how Waldo would have given her the job had she followed through on her end.

"Is this what you found out today?" Rudy asked.

"Yeah. Lauren told her dad that she was going to be

promoted to assistant principal." Could she have lied about that to her father? But he said she was the happiest he'd seen her in a while.

"I didn't know she had a father around here?" Monica said. "She never talked about family."

"She visited her dad at the retirement home once a week. He's devastated." I sipped my wine.

"Did you…" Rudy stopped and leaned back as our dinner arrived. Once we were all content with what was put in front of us, I dug in.

"Did you manage to get anything out of Carson?" Rudy asked, cutting into his steak.

"I had a nice visit with him and his wife, Carla. Did you know they are related by marriage to Sheriff Skala?" I turned my plate to get to the rice pilaf before it grew cold.

"I didn't know that," Rudy said, forking a bite of steak into his mouth.

"Did they say anything about the dinner the night before with me and Rudy?" Monica asked, with a wrinkled brow.

"No, that didn't come up. They also didn't really clear either Kyle or Viola, but they were the first people I've talked to, besides Mr. Roman, who weren't lying." I shoved rice into my mouth and savored all the herbs and spices.

"You think everyone else has been lying?" Rudy asked, putting down his knife and fork and picking up his beer.

"I know they have. Tom and Sheila were too obvious in the way they told me things or let things slip. And Waldo left out a lot of important information." I liked the three people, but one of them could be a killer.

Monica stared at me. "You think one of them did it?" she whispered.

I shook my head. "I don't know that, but I know they weren't telling me the truth. The truth is the only way to find out who did it." I circled the rim of my glass with my finger again, thinking. "I'm going to talk to the vendors near the Santa area again tomorrow. There has to be something one or more of them saw that will help get to the bottom of this. As well as visiting with my three liars."

"Do you need backup tomorrow?" Rudy asked.

I laughed and said, "No. I have to report to the sheriff in the morning about this visit with you two—"

"We're not suspects, are we?" Monica asked on an inhale of breath as her hands went to her chest.

"No. He wanted to know what you had to say about the assistant principal promotion. Then I'll see if he'll take me along to talk to Waldo again. Maybe with law enforcement involved in the questioning, he'll tell us the truth. We do know he was sitting in Hop On Inn at the time of Lauren's death."

Rudy shook his head. "What time was she killed?"

"Between four and seven, I think. I'll text Sheriff Skala and ask. Why?" I pulled out my phone, found Jason's number, and texted him. *What is the time of death for Lauren?*

"Because I saw him at the tree lighting talking to Sheila when we first arrived," Rudy said.

4-6 is the time frame, why? Jason texted back.

Rudy said he saw Waldo at the tree lighting when we arrived, which was about 6:45. What time did the barman say Waldo was at the brewpub?

He said after everyone else left for the tree lighting.

More to ask him tomorrow. See you then.

I sent a thumbs-up emoji.

"What did he say?" Rudy asked.

"Four to six. And the manager at the brewpub said Waldo was there after everyone left for the tree-lighting." I studied my empty wine glass. "He could have been there during the time of death and then went to the pub after you saw him talking to Sheila."

Rudy and Monica's eyes were wide as they both nodded.

"Don't say a word of what we talk about to anyone," I hastily said. Monica didn't need to go to school the next day and say the principal could be a killer, and Rudy didn't need to mention any of it to his buddies.

They both nodded and picked up their drinks.

"Would anyone like some dessert?" the waitress asked as she cleared away the plates.

I glanced at the two sitting across from me. "Do you want anything else?"

Monica glanced at Rudy and said, "I'd like to try their molten lava cake."

"We'll have three molten lava cakes," I ordered and smiled at Monica. It seemed she was a chocoholic like myself.

❀ ❀ ❀

By the time I returned home, the wine and chocolate had me wide awake. I decided to see what I could find out about the three people I believed were lying. The two big dogs went out for a last trip, and I settled on the couch with my laptop.

First, I looked up the Auburn school district superintendent. The name didn't ring a bell. But it was a woman. Not someone that Lauren would have snuggled up to. That meant if Waldo had promised her the assistant principal job, he would have had to go to the superintendent and plead the promotion. I didn't see that happening. And how did he think he could make Lauren believe he could give her the job? From what Monica said, any teacher would know how the hierarchy of the school system worked.

I typed in Tom Graham, Mayor of Auburn. His photo and bio appeared first. He grew up in Auburn, went to college, and returned. He married his high school sweetheart, and they took over his family's printing business. These days, he spent half his time at the business and half being mayor. Tom didn't seem to have any negatives, but he'd been holding back when she talked to him. He'd been too adamant that he would never stray.

Next, I typed in Sheila's name. Some newspaper articles popped up with her name. She was on the school board. I sat back and thought about that. Could Waldo have used his sister on the school board as a way to make Lauren believe he could make her assistant principal? She was also in an article about the lighting of the tree. I settled back on the couch and read the article. Sheila had overseen the lights being put on the tree. She'd helped unroll each string and check the lights. Had she been so involved with the lights for the tree the year before? This was Tom's second year being mayor.

I typed her name, tree lighting, and last year's date. Nothing came up. Something to think about.

I felt for Waldo wanting someone to love him who didn't want anything to do with him. But he had lied to me and to Lauren. I didn't like liars. One of the reasons Nina and I didn't get along and I didn't like Viola. I had caught them in so many lies when we were growing up that I wondered if anything truthful came out of their mouths. I credited David for how well Bailey and Todd, her brother, turned out.

Typing in Waldo's name, a bio from the school website and some articles from the newspaper came up. He'd been the principal at Auburn High for eight years. Before that, he was a math teacher. How did a nerdy math teacher become a principal? He must have taken the extra classes in the summer and applied when there was an opening. But he didn't have boss written on him anywhere. He was more of a minion.

Yet, reading the articles about all he'd done for the high school, students and teachers, he seemed to be a person who liked to keep up with the times.

The obituary for his wife popped up. I read through it. No children. His wife was the daughter of the owner of a well-known corporation in the state. They had money, and it appeared they'd traveled every summer when she was alive. If they did that, when did he take the classes to become a principal? Another question to ask him.

Athena woofed to be let in. I strode over to the door, letting her and Cocoa in.

Returning to the couch, I pulled the laptop back on my lap.

Cocoa put her head on the couch next to me and peered up with her brown eyes.

I put a hand on her head. "Yes, I'm coming to bed.

I just need to make a note of the questions I need to ask each of these people tomorrow."

Chapter Twenty-one

Thursday morning, while drinking coffee and eating my breakfast, I planned out my day. I needed to be at the sheriff's office at 10 am and at the hospital at 2 pm with the dogs. Did I take them with me all day or run home and get them before the hospital visit?

As I dressed, I decided to see if Mom minded if I left the dogs at work with her while I went to the sheriff's office. Walking out to feed the outside animals and let them into their runs, I dialed Mom.

"Good morning, Andi. Will you be coming in to work today?" Mom asked.

"Later in the day or possibly mid-day. I was asked to come to the sheriff's office and fill him in on what I found out yesterday. Could I leave the dogs with you at the wool shop while I'm at the sheriff's office? We have our usual visit to the hospital in the afternoon. I might be able to squeeze some bookkeeping in between."

"You know your dogs are fine at the shop. They

greet people and make them smile. Bring them by when you need to. I'll see you then." Mom ended the call.

I stared at the phone before I walked over and checked on the chickens. I was surprised she didn't ask me about the investigation.

She and Rudy drove by as I filled water buckets for Sparky and Cupcake. That's why she didn't ask. Rudy probably told her everything he knew from our dinner last night.

When the animals were all cared for, I loaded up the dogs and we headed to town. By the time I dropped them off at the wool shop and drove to the sheriff's office, I'd be right on time.

Leading the dogs into the wool shop, I encountered Viola and Nina whispering in the corner by Nina's spinning wheel. I ignored them and walked over to where the dog beds were laid out in a row. It was obvious Mom was happy to have the dogs.

"There you three are. I set out your beds, filled the water dish, and may even have hidden a few treats around the store." Mom winked at me, and I laughed.

"You spoil my dogs," I said and unhooked the leashes. "I stopped at the park and let them take care of business before we walked up here. They should be good for several hours."

"You know why I like having them here? They get me up and moving when they need to go out." Mom patted their heads as they all lay in their beds. She then nodded toward Nina and Viola before walking me to the back door.

We stepped out into the back alley, and Mom said, "They've had their heads together like that for nearly twenty minutes. I'd like to know what they are talking about that no one else should hear."

"They have been that way for years. As a kid, I'd try to hear what they were saying, and they'd hurt me. I later gave up caring." I pulled the collar of my coat up to stop the cold air going down my neck. "You should get back in there before you get too cold."

"I'm going in before my dentures fall out from my teeth chattering." Mom hugged me.

"I'll be back before I need to be at the hospital. But I'm not sure when. Sheriff Skala made it sound like after I fill him in, we'd talk with Waldo."

Mom shook her head. "I hope he didn't do something stupid. His wife, Millie, kept him in line when she was around. I thought Sheila was keeping an eye on him after his wife died."

I opened the door and ushered Mom back inside out of the cold. "What do you mean stupid and them keeping him in line?"

Mom rubbed her hands up and down her arms and said, "In school, he was gullible. A lot of the boys and some of the girls would play cruel jokes on him, getting him in trouble. If Sheila found out, she'd step in and stop what was going on. As an adult, it was Millie who stopped him from making poor investments, poor judgment of character, and the like. After she passed, I assumed that Sheila would have to go back to keeping an eye on him. And I think she is."

I hugged Mom and rubbed her arms. "Go back in there and wrap up in one of your afghans."

It was 9:55. I needed to hustle to get to the sheriff's office. I wasn't going to make it by 10. I hoped Jason would understand my tardiness.

❊　❊　❊

I walked through the station door at 10:10 and told the receptionist the sheriff was waiting for me. She buzzed me through. I walked down the hall to the door with the plaque SHERIFF JASON SKALA. The door was open, so I walked in.

Jason looked up from the keyboard. "Were the animals being unruly this morning?" he asked, leaning back in his chair.

"No more than usual. I'm late because I dropped the dogs off at the wool shop. Mom was telling me about Waldo."

He put his forearms on his desk and studied me. "Anything I should know?"

"I'm not sure. She said that Waldo was gullible as a boy, and Sheila would stand up for him until he was married. Then his wife made sure he didn't do stupid things. Now that she's gone, Mom said she figured Sheila was back watching out for him." I saw the moment he was thinking what I was thinking.

"He promised Lauren more than he could give her because she led him on," Jason said, picking up a pen and pulling a notebook over in front of him. "Do you think she killed Lauren to keep her brother from looking like a fool?"

"That's what I'm thinking. She was in charge of the tree lighting this year. According to the newspaper, she spent all day at the tree with the crew putting the lights on. She would have been able to make sure there was a string of lights the right height to use to strangle Lauren." I leaned forward. "We'll need to see if we can get Waldo to tell us how he planned to follow through on his promises to Lauren and see if he caves about his sister's involvement."

"Before we go after him, what did you learn from Monica last night?"

"No one at the school knew about Lauren being promoted. She said if that had happened, there would have been a lot of angry people. Lauren never took any of the summer classes needed for promotion. Monica also said the superintendent picks the principal and assistant principal, not the principal." I leaned back in my chair. "I don't know how Waldo was going to pull it off. I looked up the superintendent. She would have looked at Lauren's file and laughed at him. Possibly took his job away."

Jason rolled his chair away from his desk and stood. "Looks like we need to talk to Waldo." He walked to the coat rack by his door, grabbing his jacket and hat.

I stood and walked out the door when he motioned for me to go ahead of him. Walking down the hall, I hoped Bailey didn't pop out of a room. We made it all the way to the parking lot when her county vehicle pulled in next to Jason's pickup.

Bailey stepped out of her vehicle and asked, "Where are you two headed?" Her eyes twinkled.

"We're going to talk to a suspect. While I'm gone, could you round up Tom and Sheila Graham? I'd like them waiting for me when I get back." Jason opened his door and nodded for me to get in.

I shrugged and slid into the passenger side of his vehicle.

Pulling out of the parking lot, Jason said, "You're right, she's trying to put us together as a couple."

"Not that I would mind, but I'm not ready to go

that distance yet." I glanced over and he nodded without taking his eyes off the road. There, that was cleared up. It wasn't that I didn't like him. I wasn't ready. And I wasn't sure when or if I would be. Mick had swept me off my feet in college. I felt like they never really touched the ground until the day the garda told me he was dead. Then I came down like a twenty-ton boulder.

At Waldo's house, Jason parked and shifted his attention to me. "Let me do the talking, but if there's something I miss or that needs clarification, hop into the conversation."

I nodded, unbuckled, and stepped out.

We walked up the sidewalk to the front door, and Jason rang the doorbell.

"I had to knock last time to get his attention," I said.

Jason banged a fist on the door twice, and we waited.

Nothing.

"Was his car parked out here last time?" Jason asked.

"No. I figured it was in the garage."

"Stay put, I'll see if there is a window into the garage." Jason left me standing on the front porch and headed around the other side of the garage.

I lay my head and ear against the door and listened. It was quiet, just like the last time I was here and he'd answered.

"The car isn't in the garage," Jason said, motioning for me to meet him on the sidewalk.

When we were both in the county pickup, I said, "Can you find out what he drives? We could see if he's at Sheila's, or the school, or the brewpub."

Jason opened a laptop and started typing.

I studied Waldo's house and the house next door. An older man stood on his front porch watching us. "I'll be right back," I said and slipped out of the vehicle. I walked down the sidewalk and up to the man standing on his porch.

"Good morning. I'm working with the Sheriff's Office, and we're trying to find Waldo. Would you happen to know where he is?"

He studied me. "How come you don't have a uniform?"

"I'm a plainclothes detective. I can have Sheriff Skala come over if you'd rather talk to him." I said, raising my arm to motion him over.

"No need for that. Normally, I'd say Waldo was at the high school, but this week he hasn't been going to work. Norm down at the barber shop said he's seen him going to the Goldminer every day late morning and leaving around three."

"Thank you. Can I have your name for the record?" I asked, thinking that made me sound more official.

"Gerald Runkel."

"Thank you." Walking back to Jason's pickup, I couldn't conceal the smile. I'd just helped the investigation along.

When I slid in and buckled my seat belt, Jason asked, "Why are you smiling like you won the lottery?"

"I know where Waldo is. According to his neighbor, Gerald Runkel, he has been frequenting the Goldminer bar every day, nearly all day. He knows this because Norm at the barber shop next door to the bar has seen him going and leaving."

"Good work. I also know that he drives a two-thousand-seven Toyota Corolla. Silver." Jason started the pickup and backed out of the driveway. "Where is the Goldminer? I don't remember seeing it on the main drag."

"It's on a side street. Turn left at the Credit Union and it will be midway down the block." I wondered if Waldo was drowning his sorrows over losing Lauren or trying to forget he killed her.

Chapter Twenty-two

Walking into the dark interior of the Goldminer Bar was like stepping into a 1960s spaghetti western. The walls resembled barn wood, the tables were low, round, and mismatched, as were the chairs. The bar had stools, but the four men standing at it weren't using them. The faux lanterns hanging from the ceiling gave off different watts of light. Under the dimmest glow sat Waldo at a table in the corner.

I pointed and Jason nodded. We walked over, Jason first. He sat in the chair on the side that would keep Waldo from leaving and motioned with his head for me to sit on the other side of him.

Once we were seated, Waldo raised his gaze from his glass to us. It was hard to imagine this man as a high school principal, as low as he'd fallen in such a short time.

"Waldo, we'd like to ask you some questions. Are you clearheaded enough to give us answers?" Jason

asked.

Waldo nodded and said a slurred, "Sure."

Jason turned to me. "Go see if you can get him a cup of coffee."

I nodded and approached the bar. The woman behind it looked familiar but I couldn't place her.

"Andi? Andi Weber?" she asked, smiling.

It was the smile that made things click. "It's Andi Clark now. How are you, Clara? What are you doing working at the Goldminer?"

"Long story. What are you doing walking in here with the hot new sheriff?" She wiggled her eyebrows.

I laughed. "I'm helping him with an investigation. Do you happen to have a cup of coffee back there we can give to Waldo? We need to ask him some questions."

"Sure. Just a second." She put down the cup she was polishing and walked through swinging doors to what I figured was the kitchen.

I glanced over at the table where Waldo and Jason sat. They didn't seem to be talking.

The doors swung toward the bar, and Clara walked out with a steaming cup of coffee. "Here you go. When you get a chance, come back in and we can catch up."

"I'd like that. Thanks for the coffee." I carried the coffee back to the table, happy I'd run into another person from my childhood. Catching up with friends and being close to my family had made my decision to move back to Auburn after Mick's death.

I set the coffee near Waldo as Jason slid the alcoholic drink in front of Waldo across the table.

Waldo cupped the mug in his hands and raised it to his lips. He sipped, licked his lips, and sipped again.

"Waldo, we have some questions to ask you," Jason started. "We're having trouble with the timeline. It makes you look guilty of killing Lauren."

The man's hands wobbled and he spilled coffee. Nearly dropping the cup, if Jason hadn't grabbed it when Waldo spread his hands and started rubbing them with his shirttail.

Raising his bloodshot eyes from his hands to Jason, Waldo said, "I didn't kill her. But I wished something would happen to her and the next thing I knew, she was dead."

"Why did you nominate her for Teacher of the Year and promise her she would be assistant principal?" I asked, giving Jason an apologetic shrug. I thought his going with 'why did you kill her' first was too much for Waldo in his state.

"Payment. She was going to tell everyone. I had to give her what she wanted to keep her quiet."

I glanced at Jason. What did she have on Waldo that would make him resort to promises he couldn't keep?

"Did you tell anyone about this blackmail?" Jason asked. He had his notebook out and was writing down everything. I glanced down at his neat penmanship. He'd written *accomplice*.

Waldo shrugged. "I don't want to get anyone else in trouble. I did it, I caused the problem."

"What did you do?" I asked in a gentle voice.

"She, Lauren, caught me gambling on the school computer. When she tried to get money from me, I showed her my bank account. I have nothing except the house and what I make as a principal. I've lost it all gambling since my wife died. She said if I didn't have money, I needed to use my position to get her recognition. The Teacher of the Year was easy. I nominate the teachers. It didn't sit well with the other teachers, but what could I do? I didn't want to lose my job. It's all I have for an income." He picked the coffee back up and swallowed a large gulp. It must have cooled off.

"How did you expect to get her the assistant principal job when the superintendent picks the person?" Jason asked.

"I don't know. I asked Sheila what she thought I should do. She told me I was an idiot and had better tell the superintendent about my gambling before Lauren did." Waldo took another swallow of coffee. "I can't face anyone. Not now."

"Did you tell the superintendent?" Jason asked.

Waldo shook his head. "No. I asked Sheila about it right before the tree-lighting ceremony. That's when she told me to tell the superintendent before Lauren did. Sheila said if I got fired, she and Tom would find me a job." He moaned and said, "She's been cleaning up after me our whole lives."

I glanced over at Jason. If Sheila had cleaned up his problem, why would she have told him to tell the superintendent? Jason seemed to be contemplating the same thing from his wrinkled brow and pen sitting still on his pad.

"If you haven't told the superintendent yet, why have you been avoiding the school?" I asked.

"The teachers all think I'm spineless or worse, that I was lusting after Lauren. That was bad enough, but if they knew I'd used school equipment to lose my life savings gambling, they'd hate me even more. I have a dedicated group of teachers. They would be shocked and then furious over what I've done." He rubbed a hand over his bald head, dislodging the comb-over. It flopped down the right side of his head.

Jason shot a wide-eyed glance at me.

I had trouble not chuckling.

"I can't face them, the students, the custodians, the parents, anyone I've known through the school." Waldo stared into his coffee.

"I want you to come down to the station with me. I'll get what you've told me written up and then you'll need to sign the statement." Jason stood, taking Waldo by the arm and helping him out of the chair.

"Do you want me to walk back to the station or go to work at the wool shop?" I asked.

"You can go to work. I'll have Bailey sit in on my conversations with Sheila and Tom." Jason and Waldo left the bar.

I walked over to the counter to speak with Clara.

"Why is the sheriff taking Waldo away?" Clara asked, concern in her voice.

"He made a statement. Sheriff Skala wants to get it on record and have Waldo sign it." I sat on the stool and asked, "Did you happen to know the school teacher who was killed in the park last Saturday night?"

Clara leaned on the bar and asked in a quiet tone, "Is that what Waldo's statement is about?"

"Kind of. He didn't kill her, but his actions may have led to her death."

"Waldo?" she said with surprise.

"She seems to have been good at blackmail. Did she ever come in here with anyone?" I asked.

"Yeah, many times. The way she dressed, I was

surprised to find out she was a teacher. Always short dresses, high heels, and a neckline that didn't leave any surprises to what lay beneath the tight-fitting top." She chuckled. "I thought she was a hooker the first time I saw her. Harold, the owner of the bar, told me she taught at the high school. Made me curious if she dressed like that at school. If she did, all those hormone-infused teenagers would have had trouble concentrating in her class."

I laughed at that vision and then sobered and asked, "Do you know who she came in here with? Was it a different man every time?"

"The men seemed to only last a couple of months, and then she'd be with a new one. Her latest is none other than our esteemed mayor. He didn't put his hands all over her like the other men did when they were here. He was polite, held her chair, ordered for her, and took her coat off and put it on when they left." Clara slid a glass of water across the counter to me. "But I haven't seen them in here for several weeks, now that I think of it. She hasn't been in here with anyone for a month."

"Did she ever come in here with Kyle Stevens?" I shouldn't have asked and put the notion in Clara's head that he would be unfaithful to Viola, but I wanted to know. I still hadn't crossed the couple off my list of suspects.

"Mister of the perfect couple? No, he hasn't ever set foot in here since I started bartending ten years ago." She leaned back across the bar and asked, "Was he one of the teacher's men?"

Telling her would get rumors going around about how the Auburn Royal couple weren't so perfect, but it could also come back to bite me in the butt if Nina or

Viola learned I had spread the truth. I shook my head. "I was just curious. Nina and Viola are still friends and still treat me like a second-class citizen, so I was just curious."

Clara slapped the towel on the bar and said, "They were always mean to you in school. I can't believe how you shrugged off the things they said and did. You know why you were never asked out on dates, don't you?"

Shaking my head, I had always wondered why no boy would ask me out or even talk to me. I was young and naïve when I went off to college. I learned quickly that there was nothing wrong with me when the college boys started hitting on me. All through high school, I thought I was ugly and nerdy, and that's why I never got asked to dance or asked out on a date.

"They spread the rumor around that you came up with something that could make a male infertile if he made you upset." Clara laughed. "Now that is the stupidest thing I've ever heard, but you know how kids are in high school. The boys all believed it."

I stared at Clara. "Why didn't you tell me this if you knew?" I had spent four years of my life thinking I wasn't worthy of having a boyfriend. If it hadn't been for my nerdy girlfriends, I could have been one of the teen suicides.

She shrugged. "There weren't a lot of boys to choose from. And hey, look at you. You got out of here and captured a good man. I stayed here, married Sean Simmons, and am now a divorcee with bills to pay that my stupid husband ran up before leaving me."

"Then they did me a favor by making me think I was unworthy of the male species ever looking at me as anything but a nerd." I shoved the water glass back across the bar and walked out of the building without looking back. There were many reasons why I fell in love with Mick and didn't look back when he offered to take me around the world. While my parents were loving and caring, my big sister had ruined much of my childhood. Rudy had always stuck up for me, but he was five years younger and didn't always know what was wrong.

Shoving my hands deep into my coat pockets, I walked with my head down, not really knowing where I was headed. My thoughts tumbled around in my head as my feet registered sidewalks and streets as I crossed one block to the next.

"Hey, watch where you're going!" A voice I knew said, as I barely clipped someone on the sidewalk.

I glanced up and grabbed Betty by the arm. "I'm sorry. It's Andi. I had my head down, feeling sorry for myself and not watching where I was going."

She patted my shoulder. "It's okay. What has you distracted?"

I told her about my encounter with Clara and what I'd learned.

"Incidents in our childhood can make us bitter or joyous," Betty said. "You have learned to ignore the ones that make you bitter. That's what I always loved about you. How you could turn a cheek to your sister and Viola."

"I still don't understand why most of my encounters with Nina were bitter. All of my encounters with the rest of the family were joyous." I stopped and peered into Betty's eyes. "One of the reasons I dragged out coming back to Auburn after Mick's death was because Nina lived on the farm and was part of the family business.”

“Having heard her bitterness toward you, I understand. I’m sure your mom understands, too. It’s hard for you to work in the same space with her, even if she is your sister.”

“What’s most frustrating is I don’t know why she hates me.” I finally said out loud what I’d been skating around my whole life.

“You may never know until you sit her down and ask her. Remember I said her aura was about fear of loss and suffering. I would bet something happened when you both were small that started those feelings in her.” Betty started walking, and I fell in step beside her.

“When Mom offered me the bookkeeping job and said I could make my own hours and even work when no one was in the shop, I decided it was time to come home,” I said, as we stopped on the sidewalk not far from the Pavilion at the park. “Mick and I had talked about the way Nina treated me for hours. Neither one of us could figure out why she was so mean. He told me I needed to sit down and ask her. But she is never in the sit-down and talk mood when I’m around.” I hugged Betty. “But since my two best friends have suggested that’s what I do, I’ll see if I can make her sit down and talk to me.”

Betty smiled. “That’s a good idea. If you need someone to talk to afterwards, you know where to find me.” She straightened her Thanksgiving-decorated hat and headed down the street, her colorful cane tapping out a cadence on the cement.

The park had always been one of my favorite places. As a child, I enjoyed the swings and the slide.

As an adult, I liked the trees, the squirrels, and my dogs' excitement when they walked here.

I glanced at my phone. Nearly noon. I'd swing by Bow Wow Brew to grab a drink and a sandwich, then go to the wool shop and put in an hour or so before taking the dogs to the hospital.

Chapter Twenty-three

When I arrived at the wool shop it was just Mom, the dogs, and two customers. I set my lunch on the counter, patted the dogs on their heads, and went to the cash register to help Mom.

"Andi, these are two of the best knitters in the state," Mom said, introducing me to the women who were younger than her but older than me.

"Your family makes the prettiest colors and finest yarn in Oregon. We always tell our friends they need to come here at least once to see the whole process," one of the women said, fingering the wool in her bag.

"All the creative genius is my mom, brother, and sister's doing. I just crunch the numbers," I said, helping bag the other woman's purchases.

"Thank you for coming in," Mom called out cheerfully as the women left the shop. "Whew, I'm glad you showed up. I was beginning to think I'd be here alone all day."

"Where are Rudy and Nina?" I asked, walking to the table and laying out two napkins. I placed half the sandwich I bought on each napkin and made two cups of tea as Mom collapsed in a chair and sighed.

"Thank you for bringing lunch. I didn't bring anything with me today, thinking I'd slip out, walk the dogs, and get something." Mom picked up half of the sandwich and took a bite as I placed a cup of tea in front of her.

"You didn't answer my question. Where are Nina and Rudy?" I sat and studied her as she finished chewing and wiped her mouth.

"Rudy ran home to help David and Todd with the sheep. Nina left with Viola this morning and hasn't been back." She picked up the teacup and said, "I'm worried that woman is getting her into trouble."

I had the same thought. "I wish I could stay, but the dogs and I have to head to the hospital in an hour."

"At least I'll have company while I eat lunch." Mom smiled and picked up her sandwich.

"You were right about Waldo," I said to take Mom's mind off of Nina.

"I was? How?" Mom continued eating as I told her about Waldo's gambling and being blackmailed.

"That woman was awful the more I hear about her." Mom set the sandwich down and drank tea. She put the cup down and peered at me. "How many people do you think she was blackmailing?"

"I've been wondering the same thing. I also talked to Clara Baxter, well I guess Simmons now, at the Goldminer. That's where we found Waldo. She said that Lauren had been a frequent visitor to the bar with many men, and that until a month ago, she was showing up with Mayor Graham. Though she made it clear that he never fawned all over Lauren like the other men. But wouldn't that make for a juicy scandal right now, considering what has been coming out about the dead woman?" I picked up my sandwich to take a bite and saw the look of 'aha' on Mom's face. "What?" I asked.

"Sheila was complaining at the last Chamber meeting about how many night meetings Tom had been having lately. She asked the chamber members if they'd had any night meetings with her husband."

"She was trying to find out where he'd been. Was the owner of the Goldminer there?" I asked.

"Harold Taylor? I'd have to look at the Chamber meeting notes to be sure. He comes sometimes, so I'm not certain. You think he might have told Sheila about Tom and Lauren?" Mom sucked in a breath and said, "If he did, I'm pretty sure there was a showdown."

"If he didn't and the first time Sheila heard about it was from Lauren, she wouldn't have had time to rig up the lights," I said, thinking out loud.

"You think she helped with the lights on the tree as an excuse to set up the murder?" Mom held her hand to her throat and stared at me with scared eyes. "That would be a side of Sheila that no one would have seen."

"But what about Tom?" I asked. "He could have told Lauren to get lost and she turned around and threatened to blackmail him and if he didn't come through, she'd tell everyone he'd been cheating on his wife."

Mom shook her head. "He wouldn't have fallen for blackmail. He would have either told Sheila himself or denied it. It would have been his word, the mayor, or that of the woman who had ruined lives with lies."

I nodded as Lulu whined. "You want to close the shop for thirty minutes and go for a walk with the dogs and me?"

"I'll stay here and keep things open. Rudy should be returning soon. You didn't get any bookwork done today," she said, pointedly looking at my desk piled with receipts.

"I'll be here first thing in the morning and get it done." I hooked the leashes on the dogs and led them out the front of the shop. Standing on the sidewalk, I scanned the street. It looked the same as any other day in the first week of December. However, while I was glad I came back, I was now getting a glimpse of why I'd stayed away. So many secrets and lies could be covered up in a small town but not completely. There was always someone who was willing to tell the truth, and that usually made them the outcast.

I started down the sidewalk with Cocoa, Athena, and Lulu. While I stood, staring down the street, Lulu had peed in the dirt at the base of the tree in front of the Wool Shop. She was now trotting happily along, her tail up high, swinging back and forth like a black feathery flag.

At the park, I walked around to let Cocoa and Athena relieve themselves and found myself standing behind the unlit tree. I stared up at the strings of lights and then down at the ones that would be within reach of someone thinking about killing a person.

The string that had been the murder weapon must have been removed and replaced with a new string. I stepped up next to the tree. One set of lights was down too low to not become obvious that someone was grabbing the lights. But the string above my head… I reached up and still had about six inches before I could touch them. That meant someone taller, say closer to six feet, would have had to reach up, grab the string, and draw it around Lauren's neck before tightening it. I wondered if she was lying completely on the ground or if the string of lights had held her up slightly.

My phone beeped. I needed to get going or we'd be late for the hospital.

Before stepping away from the tree, I texted Jason. *I have more information.*

When he didn't text right back, I wondered if he was still questioning Sheila and Tom.

❀ ❀ ❀

Leaving the hospital after taking the dogs around to visit with the patients, my phone beeped. I glanced down and saw that Jason had texted.

What information?

Are you at the office?

No. Cheesy Pie. There's plenty of pizza.

10 minutes. I texted back and headed to the only pizza place in town where you could actually walk in, order, and sit down to eat. All the others were take-and-bake places, which I thought would have been more Jason's style.

"Sit tight, and I'll take you home after I've told Jason what I know," I told the dogs as they looked at me with sad eyes. I knew they wanted to go home and run around loose.

Stepping through the door of Chessy Pizza, I scanned the seating area. Jason waved a hand, and a person across from him turned their head. It appeared he was having an early dinner with his son.

I walked to the booth, and Jason slid over. Glancing at his son, I didn't see any hostility, only curiosity. Before sitting next to Jason, I held out my hand. "Hi, I'm Andi Clark."

He shook hands. "I'm Noah. His son."

I nodded, thinking he had a strong grip, and sat, putting my purse between Jason and me.

"There's plenty of pizza, grab a slice if you're hungry," Jason said.

My stomach growled at that moment. "I gave half my lunch to Mom. She was stuck at the shop. Rudy and Nina abandoned her." I grabbed the napkin Jason set in front of me and then grabbed a slice of Rudy's favorite pizza.

"Why did they do that?" Jason asked, picking up his glass of what looked like soda.

"Nina went somewhere with Viola, and Rudy had to go home and help with the sheep." I bit into the pizza, enjoying the mixture of flavors and textures. Everything But The Kitchen Sink was filled with meats, cheeses, olives, pickles, tortilla chips, and pineapple. It was not for a finicky eater.

"Sounds like you could use some help," Noah said, grabbing another slice of pizza. He didn't look at her, kept his eyes on the food.

"I heard you are a bit of an artist," I said.

His gaze rose to my face. "I like to draw and use pastels."

"Can you count money, and would you be willing to learn how to make colors from natural sources?" I would have to run this by Mom, Rudy, and Nina, but it wouldn't hurt to have another person in the store when three of us seemed to be called in different directions most of the time. It would give Nina a chance to stay home and card the wool she spins at the store. Rudy could concentrate more on the weaving and helping with the flock now that Todd was interested in weaving, too.

"What kind of store do you have?" Noah asked.

"It's run by my family. We raise the sheep that we shear and then make yarn and garments from the wool." I dug into my purse and pulled out a business card. "Come by tomorrow morning around eleven. Everyone should be there, and you can see if you're interested in working either part-time if you want to continue your schooling or full-time if you're just going to concentrate on your art."

Noah took the business card and smiled. "Thanks. I'll stop by." He finished the slice of pizza and then said, "I'm going to head home. See you there." He held his dad's gaze and then left.

"Did I scare him off?" I asked, moving to the booth he'd vacated so I could see Jason when I talked to him.

"No. This is the time of day he prefers to draw. He makes some awesome drawings of the things he sees in a day. Thank you. You didn't have to offer him a job." Jason's eyes said he was grateful.

"I don't like Mom being at the shop by herself. At her age, anything could happen. I like the idea of her always having someone there. And it would free up Rudy and Nina to do more of the prep work they need to do at home. It works for all of us." I just had to get the family on board with it. I was only a part-time employee and didn't have the right to hire anyone. But I also did the books and knew we could afford an employee.

"What did you find out?" Jason asked. He waved over a waitress and asked for a glass.

The waitress handed him one from the stack she was carrying. He filled it with soda from the pitcher and slid it over to me.

"After you left with Waldo, I talked to Clara, the bartender at Goldminer. She said Lauren was a frequent visitor with many different men. But that recently she'd been coming in with the mayor."

Jason leaned back in his seat. "He lied during our conversation this afternoon. He said he had only met the woman at school functions."

"He knew her better than that. How tall is he?" I thought he was only a couple of inches taller than me.

"Probably five nine, maybe ten if he stretched. Why?" Jason leaned forward.

"I was wandering around in the park and went behind the tree where the body was found. If the lights are strung the way they were on Saturday, I believe someone closer to six feet would have been able to reach up and grab the string that killed her. Was she flat on the ground or was the string holding her up?"

He pulled out his phone and scrolled through the photos. "Her head and shoulders are off the ground. The string of lights is holding her up because they are coming from higher up." He stared at me. "How did we miss that?"

"You were trying to keep people away and secure the scene." I smiled and picked up another slice of pizza.

"None of our suspects are six feet," Jason muttered.

"I can think of two that are close," I said around a mouthful of pizza. I couldn't believe I was so hung up on putting this murder on Viola or her husband. But there it was.

"You're talking about the Stevens."

"I want to talk to the vendors who were near the Santa area again. One of them had to have seen something more than Viola walking in with a sappy smile and storming out. Which, to me, gives her ample reason to want to get rid of Lauren. Then there's Kyle's need to stay top man and have the use of Viola's money to want to keep Lauren quiet." I raised my hands as if saying, 'What more do you need?'

"You've come up with a good argument. We'll talk to the vendors tomorrow. I didn't get a chance to talk to the ones Bailey questioned. We might learn something."

I finished my drink and grabbed my purse, pushing with my feet to slide out of the booth.

"Leaving so soon?" Jason asked.

"The dogs have been cooped up either at the wool shop or in the van most of the day. I want to get them home so they can relax." I stood. "What time tomorrow do you want to question the vendors?"

"Text me when you finish showing Noah around the shop and I'll pick you up there." He grinned. "Thanks again for giving Noah a job. We had been discussing his options when you arrived. I didn't like his suggestion that he'd go back to the reservation and live with my parents. I love them, but they are too old to worry about where my son is."

"We'll keep him as busy as he wants and suggest more schooling." Walking out of the pizza place, I knew the first place the dogs and I would walk. To

Mom's for a visit with her and Rudy about hiring Noah.

Chapter Twenty-four

"I think it's a wonderful idea," Mom said when I told her about Noah and his need for a job.

When I'd arrived at her house and said we needed to talk about getting help in the shop, she'd called Nina and had her come over too.

"I don't see why we should hire her boyfriend's son," Nina said.

I shoved my hands on my hips and glared at her. "Sheriff Skala is not my boyfriend. We are working to solve who killed a woman the night of the tree-lighting ceremony. When you two left Mom alone today, I came in and found her tired, feeling alone, and hungry."

"She could have closed the store and gone for lunch," Nina said.

"And we would have lost sales from two women who drive to Auburn twice a year to stock up on our yarn for their projects," Mom said, her complexion growing redder. "Where did you run off to with Viola?

It wasn't to do anything for the shop like Rudy, who had to help David and Todd with the sheep."

Nina crossed her arms. "What I do is my own business. I'm not a child. I can come and go as I please."

"Not if you are a partner in the business," Mom said, holding Nina's gaze. "You were the one who said you wanted to be my partner. You wanted to keep the shop running. Then act like it. Be cordial to the customers and your sister, and don't run off, leaving me to run the shop all day by myself. Excluding when Rudy and Andi were there." Mom faced me. "I am the one who is left by myself. If you say we have the funds to hire Noah, then I want him hired."

"We need to vote," Nina said, moving closer to Rudy. "All in favor of hiring Noah."

Everyone raised their hand but Nina. She huffed and said, "If you knew you were going to outvote me, why did you even call me down here and ask my opinion?"

"We hadn't discussed anything before you arrived, other than Andi saying she had someone she thought would be a good hire, so I wasn't alone in the shop. I suggested we call you down to hear her out." Mom picked up the cup of tea she'd left on the arm of the couch when she'd jumped up to go toe to toe with her oldest child, who stood a good head taller than her.

"I'll be late coming to work tomorrow," Nina said, heading for the door.

"You'll be there at eleven to welcome Noah to the store," Mom said. "That's not your partner speaking, that's your mother."

Nina huffed, glared at me, and snubbed Rudy as

she strode out the door and closed it a little too hard.

"Wow! What put her panties in a bunch?" Rudy asked.

"It's just Nina," I said, putting my coat on for the walk back to my place.

"We shouldn't have to put up with that, we're family," Mom said. "She's always worse after she's been with Viola."

I snorted and said, "Can you blame her? If I had to listen to Viola all day, I'd want to bite someone's head off, too."

Rudy laughed.

Mom just looked at me. "Seriously. I think that woman is bad for Nina."

"Viola's been bad for Nina their whole lives. But Nina, for some reason, thinks the sun rises and sets by Viola. It's going to take something drastic to make her see she's tied her basket to a cold-hearted, vicious woman." I didn't mention that we were going to check up on her alibi for the time of Lauren's death the next day.

"As a small child, she was always laughing and cheerful. I don't understand what happened to take her happiness away." Mom's eyes glistened with tears. "She was happy the first few years with David, and then she became withdrawn and prickly. How he stays with her, I'll never know."

"He's been there for the kids," Rudy said. "David is what has kept them from being bitter like Nina."

I thought about what they said on the walk back to my place. I had Lulu on the leash since it was after dark and she didn't always listen to the command to come. Athena and Cocoa were trotting down the lane ahead of us, keeping an eye out for creatures of the night.

As hard as I tried, I couldn't remember a time when Nina was smiling and happy just because. I only remember seeing her smile when she opened a present or got me in trouble. Which was sad. I would have liked to have had fun memories with her to help us bond and act like sisters instead of enemies.

❀ ❀ ❀

The following morning, I hastened through my chores and loaded the dogs into the van for a trip to the wool shop to introduce Noah to the family and then meet up with Jason.

On the drive in, I wondered if Nina wouldn't show just to prove to our mom that she was the boss of herself.

I parked in the block of free parking in the middle of town and walked down to the Wool Shop. The dogs and I entered through the alley, so they wouldn't disturb anyone who might already be in the store shopping.

Walking through the back door, I heard people arguing. *Man, I hope it's not Mom and Nina still.* As I walked down the short hall that led to the storage rooms, I stopped and made the dogs hold still. It was Nina and Viola talking.

I glanced at my watch, 10:30. Where were Mom and Rudy? Noah could show up early.

"I don't care how you feel. I need you to do this for me," Viola hissed.

"It's not right. I'm tired of lying for you," Nina replied.

This was getting good. Was that why Nina was so

uptight? She was hanging onto so many lies that Viola asked her to keep.

The door jingled.

"I'll talk to you later. But you better do it." Viola said in a loud whisper.

I stepped out of the hallway in time to see Nina rubbing her arm, Noah walking toward the cash register, and Viola's back going out the door.

"Morning, Noah," I said, leading the dogs to their beds and unleashing them. I thought it best not to let Nina know I heard her conversation. But later, I was going to do my best to get her to tell me what Viola wanted her to lie about.

Mom and Rudy bustled in through the back hallway.

"We have pastries," Mom said, smiling at Noah. "Come over here where we can have a good chat."

The young man was hesitant and glanced at me. I smiled and nodded. "This is a family business. You'll be treated like family as long as you work here."

He grinned and walked over to the table.

"Tell me about you," Mom said as I walked over to my desk and started up the computer. I needed to download the employee forms I found online the night before so Noah could fill them out. I listened with one ear as Noah said he was hoping to raise money to take art classes and that he wanted a career in that field.

Rudy asked him if he'd ever used a weaving loom. Noah said no. Mom asked if he was interested in making colors from natural sources. He said he'd mixed a few with his grandmother. Nina didn't ask any questions. She just sat at the table, picking at the pastry in front of her.

I walked over with the paperwork and set it in front of Noah. "Fill this out and then I'll show you around."

Noah glanced at me, smiled, and took the pen I offered.

While he filled out the papers, I grabbed an éclair and leaned against the counter, eating it. The dogs were all watching me take each bite. You wouldn't have guessed they'd all had their breakfast before we left the house.

"Here you go." Noah rose from the table and handed me the papers.

"Thank you." I walked them over to my desk and returned, licking my fingers. I washed at the sink, filled a cup with tea, and started with the knitted and woven garments, showing Noah the finished products and working my way through the process of product to wool.

"I didn't know there was so much that went into making yarn," he said when I finished and handed him over to Mom to teach him about sales.

It was almost noon. I had to make a decision on whether to leave the dogs here or leave them in the van while I went with Jason. I opted to leave them at the shop. With four people in the store for the rest of the day, they could take them on walks.

I walked over to the counter, and in a low voice, I said to Mom and Noah. "I have to meet Sheriff Skala. I'm leaving the dogs. You two don't mind taking them out if they need to go, do you?"

Mom assured me they were no trouble, and Noah's eyes lit up at the mention of taking the dogs out.

"Thank you. I plan to be back before you close, if not sooner. I don't know how many people he plans to talk with," I said, walking to my desk and pulling on my coat and gloves. Cocoa rose to her feet. I peered into her eyes and could tell she didn't want me to leave her. She felt my agitation. She'd be a pain for Mom and everyone else if I didn't take her with me. "I'll take Cocoa."

I walked to Bow Wow Brew and texted Jason that he could pick me up there. I ordered a hot chocolate and a sandwich for me, and a dog cookie and a pup cup for Cocoa. We were eating when Jason walked into the patio.

"I figured you had a dog with you when you said you were here, but I thought it would be all three." He walked over to the counter, ordered a coffee and a sandwich, and sat down across from me.

"I left the other two at the Wool Shop. Cocoa sensed my nervousness and would have been a pain for Mom if I'd left her." I scratched Cocoa behind the ears and smiled at her.

"She's your therapy dog?" Jason asked, unwrapping his sandwich.

"Yeah. She's what pushed me into learning what makes a good therapy animal and training them. Until her, I never would have thought that some animals could feel what you're feeling and know how to calm you." I finished off my sandwich and wadded up the papers.

"Who are we talking to first?" I asked.

"We'll start at the top of the list you gave me and work our way down. Then, depending on what we learn, we'll have a chat with Kyle and Viola." Jason finished off his sandwich and picked up his coffee. "Ready to roll?"

"Yeah."

"You don't sound sure." He set the coffee down and studied me. "What's going on?"

"I overheard a conversation between Viola and my sister when I arrived at the shop. Something about Viola wanting Nina to lie for her. Nina said she was tired of lying for her."

"You think she wants your sister to be her alibi for the time of Sheila's death?" Jason asked.

I nodded. "I can't think what else it could be."

"Let's go talk to the vendors and maybe we won't have to question your sister."

I stood feeling more agitated because I didn't want to confront my sister with something I wasn't supposed to have overheard.

Chapter Twenty-five

The first two vendors didn't change their story from when Jason first talked to them. At least that's what he told me after each interview.

Mrs. Perez welcomed us into her home. "Is this still about the woman who died at the tree lighting?" she asked, sitting in a chair while we perched on the edge of her couch.

"Yes," Jason started. "You told Deputy Harper that you saw Viola going into the Santa area happy and leaving mad. What time was this?"

"Around noon. I was waiting for my husband to bring me lunch." The woman smiled. "Yes, she came out of there like a dragon. Long strides, feet hitting the ground hard, and anger making her face red."

"Did you see her any other time that day?" Jason asked.

"No. Just at noon." Mrs. Perez leaned forward. "Do you think she did it?"

"We're just making inquiries about people who were around the pavilion and Santa area."

"There were a lot of people in and out of that area. My booth was in a good spot to meet all the people who came to see Santa." She smiled.

"What about the man who was dressed as Santa, did you see him come and go?" I asked.

"Mr. Stevens? Yes. He was whistling and said hello when he arrived with his suit. After Viola stormed out of there, I heard raised voices. Then the Santa area was closed for an hour for lunch. Mr. Stevens strode out without the costume and returned around one-thirty, I think. When there was a lull in visitors to Santa, I heard raised voices again."

"Did you ever see the woman who was in charge of the Santa area?" I asked.

"I don't know who she was to know if I saw her." The woman shrugged.

Jason scrolled through his phone and showed her the photo of Lauren on the high school website.

"Oh, yes! I saw her. She went into the Santa area before Mr. Stevens arrived. She had a picnic basket and blanket. I didn't see her leave during the lunch break." The woman tapped a finger against her bottom lip. "Come to think of it, I didn't see her leave before I packed up and met my husband to watch the tree lighting."

"What time was that?" Jason asked.

"Six-thirty."

"What did the blanket look like that the woman had when she arrived?" Jason asked.

"It was a red and gold plaid. Big. Heavy looking."

Jason scrolled through his phone again and showed

it to the woman.

"Yes. That's the blanket."

"What time did you see Mr. Stevens leave?"

"He left about five with his suit." Mrs. Perez glanced at me and then back to Jason. "Are my answers helping you?"

"Yes, they are. Thank you. Please don't tell anyone what we asked you," Jason said, rising off the couch.

I followed as the woman nodded.

She escorted us to the door, and we said goodbye.

In the county vehicle, I shifted to look at Jason. "She saw him leaving with the Santa suit at five. I saw him closer to five-thirty, leaving without the suit."

"Maybe he forgot something?" Jason scrolled through his phone and held it out for me to see.

It was a red and gold blanket covering Lauren's strangled body. I swallowed, making my gaze drift down to the blanket. "Is that how she was found?"

Jason nodded. "When I talked to Sheila, she said the blanket was over the body. She grabbed the blanket to pull it off the lights, thinking that was why they weren't working." Jason pulled his phone back. "According to Mrs. Perez, Lauren brought that blanket with a picnic basket. Kyle didn't partake of the picnic for lunch if he stormed out of there. Most likely to try and appease his wife after she sees him making out with Lauren. If all the other statements are correct."

My imagination started revving up. "What if he returned, suggested they have that picnic behind the tree, and when he got her close enough to the tree, he strangled her and then put the blanket over her so no one would know she was dead?"

"It's plausible. We need to learn what his alibi is

for the time he left the park and the rest of the night. No one placed Kyle or Viola at the tree lighting. Let's go see what they have to say."

Jason put the vehicle in drive and pulled away from the curb. As he maneuvered through town to the real estate office, I searched my mind for any flash of Kyle or Viola at the tree lighting. I don't remember seeing them, but I also didn't remember seeing Nina.

The closer we got to the real estate building, my heart pumped faster. Cocoa whined and poked her head between the seats, touching me with her nose. I scratched her ear and leaned my head against hers.

"I'm okay," I whispered.

"What's up?" Jason asked, parking the vehicle two businesses down from the real estate office.

"I'm just nervous. I don't want to find out that my sister is covering for murderers." I peered into his eyes.

"Do you really think that?" Jason asked, turning off the ignition.

"It's what keeps going through my head. I didn't see either Kyle or Viola at the tree lighting, but I also didn't see Nina. Her husband, David, was there. I didn't think to ask him where Nina was. I was watching you push the button, then Cocoa dragged me around the pavilion to Sheila."

"Call your brother-in-law and ask him. We can wait here while you do." Jason settled into the seat with the keys in his hand.

I pulled out my phone and scrolled through my contacts. "I hope I don't worry him by calling. Since he married my sister, I've only called him once. It was because I couldn't get a hold of Mom or Nina." I hit the icon and it began ringing.

"Hello?" David answered.

"Hi David, it's Andi. I realized I didn't see Nina at the tree lighting with you last Saturday. Did she stay home?"

There was a pause on the other end. "I know that you are helping the sheriff with inquiries into who killed that school teacher. Are you thinking your sister did it?"

"No. I wondered if she was with Viola." I didn't want him telling my sister I thought her capable of murder. But I did believe she would give Viola an alibi, even if she hadn't been with her.

"No. She had a headache after being in the cold all day and stayed home. She was sound asleep in our bed when I got there. Todd stayed home, too. He said she went to bed at eight-thirty."

Relief flowed through me like a shot of brandy. "Thank you. I was hoping you'd say that." I ended the call and smiled at Jason. "She was home with Todd, her son, and he said she went to bed at eight-thirty because being in the cold all day gave her a headache."

"There, now you can calm down." Jason exited the vehicle.

I was happy Nina wasn't involved, but I wondered what other lies Viola had instructed her to tell. I slid out, and Cocoa whined to go with me. Maybe she needed to pee. I snapped her leash onto her harness. She jumped out, staying close to my side.

"They may not allow her in the office," Jason said when he saw Cocoa with me.

"Hopefully, they will. She whined, which means she either has to pee or she feels I need her." I shrugged. "We'll see what they do when I walk in with her." I stopped by a tree with dirt around it in front of the business next door to the real estate office. Cocoa gave the tree a sniff and looked up at me. "I guess she thinks she needs to be with me."

We continued to the real estate office. Jason held the door for Cocoa and me.

The receptionist smiled. "Are you here looking for a home?" Her gaze flitted back and forth between me and Jason.

"No, we'd like to speak with Kyle and Viola, please," Jason said.

"Viola is here, but Kyle is out with a client. I'll see if Viola can see you." The receptionist pushed a button on the desk phone and waited. She frowned. "That's funny. She just walked back to her office. Let me see if she's in the restroom."

When the young woman walked away, I leaned over her desk and said, "Kyle is showing a property at forty-five-twelve Mulberry."

The woman came back. "I can't find her anywhere. Her car is in the back parking. She must have stepped out to get a coffee."

"Where does she usually go?" Jason asked.

"This time of day, the Lazy Bean. It's a block down on the right."

"Thank you," Jason said, and we left the building, glancing to the right.

"Do we go to the coffee shop and question Viola or go find Kyle?" I asked.

"Let's find Kyle. He will have fewer people listening in." Jason strode to the county vehicle.

I hurried Cocoa over and we climbed in.

"Do you know where Mulberry is?" I asked.

"It's about two blocks over from where Noah and I live." Jason smiled and pulled into traffic. He navigated through town to Mulberry. We drove slowly down the street until I noticed Kyle's Suburban.

"There he is." I pointed out the vehicle.

Jason parked behind the Suburban.

We both got out.

Jason joined me on the sidewalk as the couple Kyle had been talking to in the front yard walked toward a car.

We approached Kyle from the sidewalk.

His face tensed before he relaxed and held a hand out to the sheriff. "I didn't expect you to be interested in this house. From what I heard, a rival agency sold you a solid house a couple blocks over."

"I'm not interested in the house. I'm interested in you. Can we go inside and talk where it's warmer?" Jason motioned for Kyle to enter the house.

He glanced around and then walked up, opened the door, and stepped inside.

There wasn't any furniture, but I didn't care about sitting down. I just wanted out of the cold wind blowing this afternoon.

"Why is Andi with you? Did you deputize her or something?" Kyle gave me that better-than-you smile that I'd grown up seeing on Viola and Nina's faces when they put me down.

"She's here as a consultant," Jason said, standing with his legs spread and holding his notebook and pen. "Tell me when you left the community center last Saturday evening and what you did after that."

"I left around five-thirty. Got in my Suburban and drove home. Viola and I had decided to have a night in.

We'd been going all week and needed some time to relax."

"You were home all night?" Jason asked.

"Yeah. We even had Chinese food delivered. I'm sure Viola can find the ticket." Kyle smiled as if he were trying to sell us a house.

I had questions I wanted to ask, but thought it would be best to let Jason do his thing first.

"Why did you storm off around noon? Witnesses say you looked upset." Jason opened his notebook.

"A kid peed on me. I had to go home and take a shower. No one told me that would happen." Kyle glanced at me and then back to Jason.

"Is that what you were arguing with Lauren about? Getting peed on by a kid?" Jason asked.

"I wasn't arguing with Lauren." Kyle's face was getting red.

"Were you mad because Viola showed up and found you making out with Lauren?" I asked, no longer able to keep the questions in.

"What? No? Who said Viola was there?" Kyle asked, his gaze popping back and forth between me and Jason. His breathing grew ragged and his hands fidgeted.

"We have a vendor who saw Viola walk into the Santa area smiling and come out as if she were ready to hurt someone." Jason added, "And right after, the witness heard you and Lauren arguing."

"Maybe that's why you left at noon. To go make peace with your wife," I said, seeing the sweat beading on Kyle's forehead.

"We know you and Lauren were sleeping together. But you were good. You managed to keep her away from anyone who would start rumors. You didn't want to ruffle Viola's feathers. She has a pretty mean temper." I couldn't stop myself. I wanted to see him crack. To hear him say he or Viola killed Lauren.

Kyle put up his hands as if warding off someone and said, "Look, I was sleeping with Lauren. We kept it on the down low. We both knew how volatile Viola can get when she's not getting her way. And yes, Viola showed up when Lauren was draped all over me. But I told Viola it was one-sided. That I didn't care for Lauren. It was flattering to have her fawning all over me." He walked backward and leaned against the island in the open floor plan. "She believed me and told me I had to tell Lauren to stay away from me or she would take care of the problem."

I glanced at Jason.

He nodded.

I asked. "I saw you leaving the festival area at five-thirty without your Santa suit, and a witness said you left at five with the suit. What did you do with the suit, and why did you return to the area and leave again at five-thirty?"

Kyle's face paled. He stared at the floor, his jaw clenching and unclenching. "I left to put the suit in my car. When I got to my car, I couldn't find my keys. I figured they must have fallen out when I put the Santa suit on. I left the suit on the hood of the car and went back to the pavilion and sleigh to look for my keys. They weren't there. I looked mad when I left because I had to figure out a way to get another set of keys."

"Was Lauren still in the area when you walked back in?" Jason asked.

"No. Her stupid picnic basket was there, but the

blanket was gone." He stared at Jason. "She thought we could have a picnic in the sleigh when we finished for the day. That wasn't a way to keep our relationship quiet."

"You didn't do a very good job of it that day. Lauren's daughter saw you kissing her mom," I said, remembering the sorrow and anger in the child's voice as she talked to Athena.

"I have a feeling more people than you think knew about what you and Lauren were doing in that sleigh between children visiting Santa," Jason said. "Do you know where Viola was from five to six p.m.?"

Kyle peered at Jason, then at me, and back to Jason. "Viola? No. I was at the park, trying to get home. I assume that's where she was. She had planned lunch with Nina and then shopping."

I latched onto that. Was that the lie Viola wanted Nina to tell? Nina was working the wool shop booth all day. "But we have an eyewitness who saw Viola at the pavilion headed to the Santa area at noon. Remember, *happy* going in and *mad* coming out?" I accentuated the happy and mad.

"Call Viola and ask her where she is right now. We need to talk with her." Jason walked over next to Kyle. "And don't say we want to talk to her or anything else."

Kyle pulled his phone out of his pocket, swiped his finger across the screen, and held it up to his ear.

"Hi, Viola." He paused. "Yes. I think they're going to buy the house. I'm done. Where are you?" He listened. "Okay. See you in a few." He ended the call and said, "She's heading home."

"Give me your phone. We'll follow you there." Jason took Kyle's phone.

We all walked out of the house, watched Kyle lock up, and get into his Suburban.

Once we were in the county vehicle following Kyle, I asked, "Is he saying his wife killed Lauren?"

Chapter Twenty-six

Jason shrugged. "Or trying to make us think she did. He had motive and opportunity, and his not finding his keys could be an excuse for going back and killing Lauren."

I nodded, hoping we weren't running into an ambush because the husband and wife killed the woman and would shut us up as well to keep their status as a perfect couple.

Jason parked behind Kyle and stepped out of the vehicle.

I hung back, making sure my door was ajar so Cocoa could get out if I called for her. I didn't trust these two. I had a history with Viola and knew she would fight to keep her status in town.

Walking quickly, I caught up and stayed behind Jason. He was a trained officer.

Kyle stopped with his hand on the handle. "I should probably go in and tell her you're here."

"No, we'll all go in together," Jason said, nodding for him to open the door.

Jason was right behind Kyle when he entered.

I waited a beat before I stepped in and closed the door.

"Kyle, let's celebrate!" Viola said, walking out of what appeared to be a sitting room. She held a bottle of champagne and wore a long dressing gown. "What are they doing here?" Her welcoming tone was now the howl of an ogre.

"We have questions for you." Jason motioned for her to go back into the room. Then he motioned Kyle to follow.

Once we were all in the room, Kyle and Viola were seated on the couch, Jason in a chair in front of them. I sat to the side on an ottoman.

Jason pulled out his notebook. "I have some questions that need answering."

"I have a question," Viola said, glaring at me. "What is she doing here?"

"Andi is consulting with me on the investigation. Where were you Saturday at noon?" Jason held his pen ready to write.

"I was having lunch with Nina." Viola narrowed her eyes. "You can call and ask her."

"We don't need to. We have a witness who saw you walking into the Santa area at the Christmas Festival around noon and storm away within minutes of entering. What did you see that made you angry?" Jason kept his gaze on Viola.

I watched Kyle.

"Your witness must be lying," Viola said.

Kyle put a hand on her knee. I saw his knuckles whiten as he squeezed it.

Viola shot a glance at her husband. He shook his head.

"They know you were at the community center. They know you saw Lauren all over me. I told them I caught up to you and we had a talk. I told you how Lauren was throwing herself at me." Kyle released her knee and picked up her hand, raising it to his lips. "You're the only woman for me."

Viola blushed, and for once, the hard angles of her face actually softened. I felt like throwing up. It was as insincere as anything I'd ever heard. I glanced at Jason. He rolled his eyes. Good, we were on the same page with this act.

I started to open my mouth to ask a question, and Jason asked, "What were you doing between five and seven p.m.?"

Viola's eyes snapped back to anger. "Why?"

"Just answer the question." Jason stared at her.

She flicked two nails together and stared out the window as if trying to remember. "I stopped off at the Chinese restaurant and brought home takeout, then changed and waited for Kyle to come home."

They were off on this. One of them was lying. Kyle had said they'd had takeout delivered.

"What time did Kyle get home?" Jason asked.

"I think it was close to seven? I wondered what was keeping him. We'd planned to have dinner and then go to the tree lighting." She glanced at her husband.

He was staring out the window.

"How did he act when he came home?" Jason

asked.

"Act? What do you mean? He said he was tired. Didn't understand how listening to children all day could make him so tired. Said he didn't feel like going back out into a lot of people. So we ate the takeout I brought home, watched a movie, and went to bed."

I jumped in. "Kyle said you ordered takeout after he got home." Viola glared at me. I shifted my gaze to Kyle. "Was Viola here when you arrived home? I know you left the community center at five-thirty, maybe a quarter to six. I saw you leaving without the Santa suit. Did you really not get home until seven, or was it Viola who didn't get home until then?"

Viola glared at me. "I didn't get home until seven, and then we ordered takeout. There, are you happy?"

"But what were you doing if you weren't at home?" Jason asked.

"If you must know, after I saw that horrible woman all over Kyle, I was angry and mortified. I couldn't believe he'd let someone like that even touch him. He caught up to me as I sat in my car, trying to make sense of it all. He told me it was all her. If he'd known that she asked him to be Santa so she could be alone with him, he wouldn't have agreed. But he loves kids. He was and is the best dad. He'll be a wonderful grandfather." Tears glistened in her eyes. "I wanted to believe him. Believe it was all her. But I know I'm not the easiest woman to be around."

"You have your moments, but you're the one I love," Kyle said, again kissing her hand.

"What did you do after you talked to Kyle?" Jason asked.

"I started to go home, but didn't want to sit alone,

wondering if he would really come home or go somewhere with that woman. So, I went to the Golden Goose bar. Tom was there. He was eating lunch, so I joined him. I knew I could count on him to be discreet. I told him what I'd seen and that Kyle said it was all her. I asked him if he thought that was true. He got a weird look in his eyes and said, 'Yeah, it sounded like what he'd heard about the woman.' We sat there a couple more hours, and he said he had to go help Sheila with the finishing touches for the tree lighting and left. I stayed through happy hour, not wanting to go home. Then Kyle called and said he was home and wanted to know where I was."

My mind started circling when she mentioned Tom and that she told him about Lauren. I made eye contact with Jason.

"Okay, thank you for answering our questions." Jason stood. I followed, and we left the house.

"Tom," I said when we were buckled into the county vehicle.

"I was hoping we'd have results back from forensics by now. We don't have any proof that he or either of these two did it. But that last part Viola said sounded like the truth." Jason started the vehicle and drove out of the driveway.

"He was seeing Lauren, treating her like a lady. Just because Clara said they hadn't been in the bar lately doesn't mean that they broke up. Jealousy could have tipped him to kill her."

"Or the fact she'd told his wife they were fooling around and then he heard she was ruining another marriage," Jason said.

"Or he knew about the blackmail of his brother-in-law. All of it could have sent him after her," I said.

Jason nodded as he drove.

"If you don't have physical evidence yet, we need to find a witness who saw him at the park. He would have been there to help Sheila. That would have given him an excuse."

"Let's ask Mrs. Perez if she saw him and then ask Sheila when Tom arrived to help her." Jason went around a block to head us in the opposite direction we'd been traveling. Mrs. Perez lived on the other side of town.

❈ ❈ ❈

"I didn't expect to see you two again so soon," Mrs. Perez said, answering her door.

"We have another question," Jason said. "Did you see the mayor go in or out of the Santa area?"

"Mr. Graham? He and Sheila were all over the place in the morning. After Sheila came out of the Santa area upset, she didn't go back." Mrs. Perez tapped her lower lip and stared across the street. "I did see Mr. Graham coming from behind the tree on one of my trips coming back from taking a tote to my car."

"What time would that have been?" Jason asked.

"Close to six? I think. It was the last tote, and I went back for my table and chair."

"Thank you. I'd like you to come down to the Sheriff's Office in the morning and sign the statement I'll have written up about both of our conversations."

"I can do that. I'm glad I could help." Mrs. Perez smiled and closed the door.

"We have a witness seeing him come from behind the tree during the time of death," I said, feeling like we

223

were getting somewhere, but sad that it looked like Tom had committed the crime.

Chapter Twenty-seven

"I'm going to wait until tomorrow to confront him. It will give more time for forensics to get the results back to me," Jason said as he pulled up in front of the Wool Shop. It was a quarter to five. I'd barely made it before the shop closed. "Don't say anything to anyone about what we now believe."

I opened the door and stepped out. "I'll keep it to myself. Do you think you'll have him in custody before the tree lighting tomorrow night?"

He shrugged. "I don't know. I hope so."

"Who will do the lighting of the tree then?" I wanted life to get back to normal.

"I'm sure someone will step up."

I motioned for Cocoa to hop out and then put the leash on her harness. "Good luck tomorrow."

"Thanks. Good night." He pulled away from the curb, and I faced the store.

Mom, Rudy, and Noah were watching me. I put a

smile on my face and walked through the door.

"How did things go today?" I asked, walking over and petting Athena and Lulu, who rose off their beds, their tails wagging.

"Good. Noah is a quick learner," Mom said, walking over to lock the door and turn the open sign.

"It's all interesting," Noah said. "What time do you want me here tomorrow?"

"We open at nine. You can work until three on Saturdays and have Sunday and Monday off. If you find classes you want to take, just let me know the schedule and we'll work with it." Mom put a hand on his arm. "I'm glad Andi suggested hiring you. I like the idea of always having someone in the store with me."

I glanced at Rudy and saw he was relieved about it, too. It wasn't just me who had noticed her slowing down.

"I'll be here. Do you want me to come in the front door or the back?" Noah asked.

"The back. Rudy will show you the code to get in. That way, if you are the first one here, you can start the kettle warming and be inside where it is warm." Mom walked to the hooks on the wall where coats were hung.

I leashed up Athena and Lulu. We all followed Rudy and Noah out the back door. I said goodnight and continued with the dogs to the parking lot. Walking, I wondered where Nina was. Had she stayed the day or left as soon as we'd hired Noah?

The dogs tugged on the leashes as I started to head to the car. Athena and Lulu had their noses pointed toward the park. Not knowing when they were last outside, I let them lead me.

The decorated tree loomed tall and dark into the

dusk. Another fifteen minutes and all the park lights would come on. The dogs tugged on the leashes, each wanting to go a different direction.

"Just do your business and we'll head home," I said, watching Lulu sniff the ground as if she were on the trail of a squirrel.

Would the community turn out for the tree lighting again tomorrow night? Or had the murder last weekend spoiled the event for everyone?

As I thought about it, the idea of another tree lighting didn't seem right. They should just turn the lights on and forget about the ceremony.

I pulled out my phone and scrolled through my contacts. Sheila popped up. I touched her name and the phone started ringing. It went to voicemail.

"This is Sheila, I'm busy at the moment, leave a message and I'll get back to you as soon as I can." The phone beeped, and I said, "Sheila, this is Andi. I've been thinking about the tree lighting. Maybe it would be best not to have a ceremony tomorrow night. Just have the city turn the lights on and give the community a sense of normalcy. Just my two cents about it. Talk to you soon."

I ended the call. "Come on. Let's go home, sit by the fire, eat popcorn, and watch a movie."

All three dogs turned their noses toward the parking lot and we headed to the van.

❄   ❄   ❄

At home, I had to check on the other animals, giving them grain, checking their water, and in the case of the chickens and rabbits, locking them in their houses for the night. Cocoa and Athena were loose, running around sniffing. Lulu wasn't happy, but it was dark, and I didn't want her wandering off and ignoring me when I called. Her leash was attached to my belt loop with a snap ring. She tugged now and then, but her ten pounds didn't budge me.

In the house, I started the propane fireplace, took a hot shower, and put on my fleece pajamas. The dogs were fed and settled in their beds as I popped corn and scrolled through the movies on my television.

I decided a comedy was what I needed and settled on one. Sitting on the couch, Lulu lying against my thigh, the bowl of popcorn in my lap, and a glass of wine on the coffee table, I started the movie.

My phone jingled. I looked at the caller. It was Sheila. I finished chewing my mouthful of popcorn and answered, "Hi Sheila."

"Why are you trying to ruin the tree-lighting?" Her voice was higher than usual.

"I'm not. I just feel, given what happened last weekend, it might be better to just quietly turn the lights on and have the whole tree lighting ceremony next year. You know, kind of out of respect for Lauren." I wasn't sure where that came from, but it sounded good.

"That woman doesn't deserve respect. You know the way she was. Running around sleeping with men when her husband and child had to hear the rumors and hide." She sucked in air and said, "This town deserves a tree-lighting ceremony if for no other reason than to cleanse their hearts."

"Okay, if you're that adamant about it. I was just saying how I felt. You can have the ceremony, I'm just not sure how many people will show up." I sighed.

Why was she being adamant about the ceremony?

Cocoa stood. Her ears were pointed as she listened. A low growl vibrated where her neck was against my knee.

"I have to go," I said, ending the call and scrolling for Jason's name. I hit the icon as the front door swung open and Tom walked in, dragging Sheila behind him.

"Tom, Sheila, what are you doing here?" I said loudly and in a panic.

Cocoa lunged at the man. He struck out with his foot, but Cocoa was athletic and outmaneuvered him.

Before I could even get off the couch, Athena lunged at him.

Cocoa had managed to get behind the man.

Between Athena hitting him in the chest and Cocoa tripping him, Tom toppled over backward.

Sheila jumped to the side.

Athena sat on Tom's chest, and Cocoa had her mouth at the man's throat.

Bailey ran up to the door, out of breath. She took in the situation and said, "Call off your dogs, I have it."

"Athena, Cocoa, heel," I said firmly.

Cocoa released his neck.

Athena slowly stepped off his body, coming to sit next to me.

Sheila had tears running down her face as Bailey pulled Tom up and put handcuffs on him, telling him his rights.

I walked over to Sheila and put my arm around her. "Why did he bring you here?"

"He said you must know something, and we needed to talk to you." Her eyes were red and her face blotchy from crying. "He did it, didn't he? He killed that awful woman."

Jason entered as Bailey pulled Tom out of the house.

"How did you get here so fast?" I asked, moving away from the distraught woman.

"I had Deputy Harper keeping an eye on Tom after our information gathering today. When she said he was headed in this direction, I figured he was coming to see what you knew. I received your call about five miles back." He put an arm around my shoulders. "Are you okay?"

I smiled and nodded to the three dogs sitting by the couch. "My cuddle crew kept me safe."

Epilogue

The next day, after giving my statement to the police and taking my dogs for a pup cup for being so heroic, we went to the Rockin' Retirement Home. I wanted to tell Lauren's dad that the person who killed his daughter had been caught.

He enjoyed scratching the dogs as I told him who had shortened his daughter's life. He thanked me and said that when I brought the dogs on Wednesday, he'd be in the lounge to greet them.

My next stop was to see Ava. I didn't want her to hear all the awful things about her mother, but I wanted her to know that the person who killed her mother was caught. She hugged me and asked if she could sit with Athena for a bit. I left her sitting in the van with Athena and went in search of her dad.

Nick was fixing fence down by a creek. He greeted me with a smile. "Did you come to talk to Ava?"

"Yes, I told her the person who killed her mom has

been caught. Then she wanted some time with Athena."
I studied him. It was as if a cloud had been lifted from
him. While he still had the lines of a man who didn't
get enough sleep, he didn't seem as depressed.

"I don't know why she can't talk to our dogs, but
all she wants to do is talk to Athena. Do you mind if I
call you now and then so she can visit?"

"That's fine. That's what my animals are for, to
help people heal."

"I know you helped the police a lot. I appreciate
that you didn't just think I did it and kept looking."
Nick peered into my eyes. "I would never kill the
mother of my child, no matter how horrible she was."

"I know that. And that's why I helped find the
answers. Will you be at the next Tree Lighting?"

"We'll see. We don't have wonderful memories
anymore."

Even though I thought not having the tree-lighting
ceremony was a good idea, the community felt
otherwise. Once word got around that the killer was
caught and it was up to the community to decide if they
wanted a ceremony, it was postponed to the following
Saturday.

Food carts set up as well as some craft booths. The
evening was even better than the night the tree didn't
light.

Jason was asked to be the master of ceremonies.
He called me up to push the button to light the tree.

Afterwards, we wandered around the booths and
tasted what the food carts had to offer. Noah and Todd
were walking around with Athena, Cocoa, and Lulu. I
noticed they had a lot of girls and women stopping to
ask them about the dogs.

When we sat on a bench away from the crowd, Jason said, "Tom confessed. When Sheila confronted him about sleeping with Lauren, he knew he'd have to do something to keep Lauren quiet and stop her from blackmailing Waldo. He didn't know what, but when Viola told him about her going after Kyle, he knew she wanted to get hold of the Stevens' money or prestige. He wasn't going to let her ruin more lives." Jason sipped his hot chocolate and continued. "He slipped into the pavilion from the back by the sleigh. Lauren was happy to see him. He spotted the picnic basket and said they could have a picnic behind the tree. They went out, he set things up, and maneuvered her back into the tree as if he were going to kiss her." Jason looked up from where he'd been staring at his cup. "You were close about the height of the killer. He said he had to stretch to grab the light string and wrap it around her neck. But the taut string helped him strangle her. Then he tossed the blanket over her and put the basket back. He said he'd do it again to save this community from her."

I listened with a sad heart. "He was willing to go to prison for life to save his constituents from that blackmailing woman. He should have just told you about her."

"That's what I said, but he felt she would have gotten a slap on the wrist and be back doing what she did here or somewhere else."

"I'm glad Viola wasn't involved. I don't think Nina would ever talk to me again if I had helped to put her away." I shivered thinking of how cold Viola was and how superficial her marriage to Kyle was. "I don't understand how she and Kyle can keep up the pretense of a wonderful marriage."

"It takes all kinds to marry all kinds." Jason finished his hot chocolate and motioned to the crowd. "Ready to go back before someone gets the idea we're more than friends?"

"Yes. I'm cold. I'm going to gather my dogs and go home. We've had enough excitement for a long time." I stood and handed my empty cup to him. "See you around, Sheriff."

I walked back to the milling people, found my dogs, and thanked the boys for hanging onto them. Then I said my goodbyes to family and friends and fondly looked forward to my bed and a peaceful night.

As I walked away from the activity, I heard my name called. Turning, I spotted Betty standing beside a park bench.

"Andi, can we talk?" she called.

"Yes." I walked back to her. The dogs wagged their tails and crowded around my friend.

Betty patted the two larger dogs' heads. "Hello. You girls are good company for Andi. I'm glad she has you." She dug into her bag and held out a package. "I wanted you to have this. I received a letter from a cousin yesterday. She wasn't in the village of my birth when I had gone there searching for family. She heard about my visit and asked if I'd like to come back. She would take me around and acquaint me with the family."

"Are you going?" My stomach knotted with dread for my friend. She said that all her family wanted was money from her.

"I told my cousin I would think about it. I have someone from the embassy checking to make sure this is really a relative. She sent me a photo. Would you look at it and see if it looks like me at all?" Betty held a letter out to me.

I took the letter. "The lighting here isn't very good. Can we meet tomorrow at J&P around ten? I'll look it over tonight when I can see it better."

"You're being cautious. I knew you would. Thank you. I'll see you tomorrow."

I held onto the letter all the way to the van. I put it on the dashboard before loading up the dogs. Once they were loaded and I had the van started, I turned on the overhead light and pulled the photo out of the envelope.

I gasped, staring into the face of my friend. Only her eyes were staring right at me with a twinkle in them. I had a feeling that whoever took her around when she went to Ethiopia hadn't taken her to her real family. They would have seen the likeness.

I would be sad to have Betty leave when we had just connected again, but I also understood my friend's desire to find family. After all, that was why I returned to Auburn.

❄ ❄ ❄

Thank you for reading book one in the Cuddle Farm Mystery series. I enjoyed creating Andi, Betty, the family members. And the therapy animals.

If you'd like to know when the next book is available sign up for my newsletter. https://bit.ly/2IhmWcm

If you enjoyed this book and haven't read any of my other mystery series, you might check out my Shandra Higheagle Mystery series, my Gabriel Hawke novels, or my Spotted Pony Casino Mystery series.

About the Author

Paty Jager grew up in Wallowa County in NE Oregon and has always been amazed by its beauty, history, and ruralness. She has always been interested in the Indigenous people and their culture. She enjoys learning more every time she writes a book.

Paty is an award-winning author of 64 novels of murder mystery and western romance. All her work has Western or Native American elements in it, along with hints of humor and engaging characters. She and her husband raise alfalfa hay in rural eastern Oregon. Riding horses and battling rattlesnakes, she not only writes the western lifestyle, she lives it.

By following her at one of these places, you will always know when the next book is releasing and if she is having any giveaways:

Website: http://www.patyjager.net
Blog: https://writingintothesunset.net/
FB Page: Author Paty Jager
Instagram - @patymjager
Goodreads:
http://www.goodreads.com/author/show/1005334.Paty_
Jager
Newsletter- Mystery: https://bit.ly/2IhmWcm
Bookbub - https://www.bookbub.com/authors/paty-
jager

Windtree
Press

Thank you for purchasing this Windtree Press publication. For other books of the heart, please visit our website at www.windtreepress.com.

For questions or more information, contact us at info@windtreepress.com.

Windtree Press
www.windtreepress.com

www.ingramcontent.com/pod-product-compliance
Lightning Source LLC
Chambersburg PA
CBHW050615190726
48283CB00007B/2427

9 781940 064109